JOHN HENRY

BOOKS BY
ROARK BRADFORD

———

OL' MAN ADAM AN' HIS CHILLUN

OL' KING DAVID AN'
THE PHILISTINE BOYS

JOHN HENRY

❧

JOHN HENRY

BY

Roark Bradford

WOODCUTS BY

J. J. LANKES

THE LITERARY GUILD

NEW YORK

1931

PUBLISHED BY

HARPER & BROTHERS

C O N T E N T S

[v]

CONTENTS

JOHN HENRY

He went to the East and he went to the West
And I reckon he went all around.
He went to the river and he got baptized,
So they laid him in the burying-ground,
Lord, Lord,
'Cause he died with his hook in his hand.

THE BIRTH OF JOHN HENRY

Now John Henry was a man, but he's long dead.

The night John Henry was born the moon was copper-colored and the sky was black. The stars wouldn't shine and the rain fell hard. Forked lightning cleaved the air and the earth trembled like a leaf. The panthers squalled in the brake like a baby and the Mississippi River ran upstream a thousand miles. John Henry weighed forty-four pounds.

John Henry was born on the banks of the Black River, where all good rousterbouts come from. He came into the world with a cotton-hook for a right hand and a river song on his tongue:

JOHN HENRY

"Looked up and down de river,
  Twice as far as I could see.
Seed befo' I gits to be twenty-one,
  De Anchor Line gonter b'long to me, Lawd, Lawd,
  Anchor Line gonter b'long to me."

They didn't know what to make of John Henry when he was born. They looked at him and then went and looked at the river.

"He got a bass voice like a preacher," his mamma said.

"He got shoulders like a cotton-rollin' rousterbout," his papa said.

"He got blue gums like a conjure man," the nurse woman said.

"I might preach some," said John Henry, "but I ain't gonter be no preacher. I might roll cotton on de boats, but I ain't gonter be no cotton-rollin' rousterbout. I might got blue gums like a conjure man, but I ain't gonter git familiar wid de sperits. 'Cause my name is John Henry, and when fo'ks call me by my name, dey'll know I'm a natchal man."

"His name is John Henry," said his mamma. "Hit's a fack."

"And when you calls him by his name," said his papa, "he's a natchal man."

THE BIRTH OF JOHN HENRY

So about that time John Henry raised up and stretched. "Well," he said, "ain't hit about supper-time?"

"Sho hit's about supper-time," said his mamma.

"And after," said his papa.

"And long after," said the nurse woman.

"Well," said John Henry, "did de dogs had they supper?"

"They did," said his mamma.

"All de dogs," said his papa.

"Long since," said the nurse woman.

"Well, den," said John Henry, "ain't I as good as de dogs?"

And when John Henry said that he got mad. He reared back in his bed and broke out the slats. He opened his mouth and yowled, and it put out the lamp. He cleaved his tongue and spat, and it put out the fire. "Don't make me mad!" said John Henry, and the thunder rumbled and rolled. "Don't let me git mad on de day I'm bawn, 'cause I'm skeered of my ownse'f when I gits mad."

And John Henry stood up in the middle of the floor and he told them what he wanted to eat. "Bring me four ham bones and a pot full of cabbages," he said. "Bring me a bait of turnip greens tree-top tall, and season hit down wid a side er middlin'. Bring me a pone er cold cawn bread and some hot potlicker to wash hit down. Bring me two hog jowls and a kittleful er whip-powill peas. Bring me a skilletful er red-hot biscuits and a big jugful er cane molasses. 'Cause my name is John Henry, and I'll see you soon."

So John Henry walked out of the house and away from the Black River country where all good rousterbouts are born.

COONJINE

COTTON was piled a mile high on the levee, both ways twice as far as you could see, the fall John Henry took to the river. He hadn't meant to take to the river, but the old woman told him, she said, "John Henry, you's a man, but yo' home ain't hyar."

"Well," says John Henry, "I b'lieve I'll be gittin' around. I got a eetch on my heel and a run-around on my weary mind. I got to scratch my feet on strange ground and rest my weary mind on a strange pillow. So fix up my bundle, old woman, and gimme my hat. 'Cause I'm fixin' to git around some."

So the old woman got his bundle and his hat. "Whar you bound to, John Henry?" she asked him. "You's a man of movements, but livin' is hard. Whar you bound to, son?"

"I'm bound, all right," said John Henry, "but I ain't made up my mind whar. I might be bound to Memphis, and I might be bound to Natchez. But f'm what de song say, I'm a windin' ball and bound to N'Awlins." And he stood up and sang the song:

"Backed up to Memphis and she turned around.
Run right by Natchez but she didn't slow down—
She give a long, keen whistle, sweet thing,
'Cause she's N'Awlins bound!"

"Dar, now!" said the old woman. "Got a steamboatin' song already, son, and you ain't started to gittin' around yit! Listen at me, John Henry. N'Awlins is too far to wawk to, and you ain't got no wings. But de steamboats has tuck many a good nigger down de river, and dey ain't never brang one back. So jest mind out!"

John Henry went to the landing where the cotton was piled a mile high. A hundred steamboats had their stages down, and a hundred niggers were rolling cotton on every steamboat. A hundred mates were cussing and a hundred drivers were bawling for the niggers to roll that cotton down. But the faster the niggers rolled, the more cotton piled up from the gins. And the more niggers that got on the stage, the more the stage would swing and spring, until they could hardly walk it down. But the driver yowled louder for more cotton, and the niggers rolled faster and sang louder:

> "Grab dat bale and make hit roll,
> Down dat gang-plank, damn my soul!"

So John Henry climbed up on top of the cotton and watched. "Look like dem bullies is workin' hard," he said. "And hit look like dey's singin' hard. But de cotton pile higher, and de plank weave and wave."

So about that time the driver of the *Big Jim White* spied John Henry sitting a mile high on top of the cotton.

"Hey, you, boy!" said the driver. "Dat ain't no way to roll cotton! Settin' on hit like a turkey buzzard on de aigs. Cotton is comin' in fast enough, widout you up dar hatchin' more out."

"When you tawk to me," said John Henry, "call me by my name. My name is John Henry; and my home ain't hyar."

"Well, John Henry," said the driver, "my name is Copperhaid, and I'm de he-coon on de *Big Jim White*. And hit takes a natchal man to roll cotton for me!"

"Efn I ain't a natchal man," said John Henry, "you show me a natchal man, and I'll mock him."

"Well, roll hit, den," said the driver. "Roll dat cotton like a natchal man!"

So John Henry got down and started to roll.

"Two men to de bale," said the driver. "A bale weighs five hund'ed pounds, and hit takes two men to swing hit."

So a big nigger named Sam got with John Henry, and they started to roll. But when Sam and John Henry and that five-hundred-pound bale of cotton all three got on the stage, it started to pitch and swing like a tree in a storm.

"Uh-uhh!" said John Henry. "Somethin' wrong dis time. When I'm on de solid ground, I'm a man and you can't stop me. But on dis hyar jumpy gangplank, I ain't got no place to set my strenk. Keeps all er my strenk busy to keep f'm gittin' bucked offn dis plank, let alone to roll de cotton."

"Ain't nothin' wrong wid de plank," said Sam.

" 'Cause dat's de way hit's made—long and springy. And hit ain't nothin' de matter wid de cotton, 'cause dat's de way hit's baled—weighin' five hund'ed pounds. So efn hit's somethin' wrong, hit must be wid you."

Well, that made John Henry mad! "Git away f'm dis cotton, Sam!" he said. "Git away, 'cause I'm gittin' mad." And when he said that he got so mad he couldn't see! So he picked Sam up and chunked him off the plank like a feather in the wind. Then he got down and laid his shoulders against the bale and heaved. And the bale rolled!

"Look at that big nigger roll cotton," said the mate. "He's a bully and you can't stop him!"

But every time the bale rolled, the plank swung and pitched. And every time the plank weaved, John Henry couldn't place his feet to get his strength behind the bale again.

"Now, I'm done got mad!" said John Henry. "I'm a man wid strenk, but I can't use hit. 'Cause ev'y time I gits ready to git set, dis plank bucks me out er place. And dat makes me mad! Now git out er my way, you bullies! 'Cause me and dis cotton goin' round and round!"

And while everybody was looking, John Henry

backed his back up against that bale of cotton, and he caught it with his fingers like a cotton hook, and he heaved! And that John Henry—that big black man from the Black River country—heaved that five-hundred-pound bale of cotton squarely on his shoulders and started to walk!

"Wrassle dat cotton, son!" said the driver. "You's a cotton-rollin' man on de *Big Jim White*, so wrassle dat cotton down. Hit's cotton and you's nigger. So wrassle hit down, son!"

And John Henry took one step!

"Wawk away, John Henry!" said the driver. "Wawk away wid dat cotton!"

And John Henry walked!

"Look at that big nigger walk with that cotton," said the mate.

"Yeah, but look at dat stage heave and pitch under his foots," said the driver. "Mind out, John Henry. Dat plank is a solid hund'ed-feet long, and she spring like a willow tree! Mind out, John Henry, or dat plank will spring you off!"

"Let de plank spring," said John Henry, "and I'll spring right back at hit. Let hit buck like a bull, and I'll buck like two bulls! Let hit jump like a high-land frog, and I'll jump like a pant'er in de brake! Let hit weave like a willow tree, and I'll weave like a feather bed! 'Cause I'm John Henry, and I aims to be gittin' around."

And so John Henry got a spring in his knees, and a weave in his hips, and a buck in his back, and the stage couldn't do him a thing!

"Look at dat bully swing along!" said the driver. "Hey, you niggers! Jine dat step. Roll yo' cotton, but jine dat tread!"

"Jine it, you coon, jine it!" said the mate. "Grab your cotton and jine that step!"

So the niggers watched John Henry until they caught his weaving step, and then they started rolling their cotton down the plank, springing and bucking right back at the plank! And the first thing they knew, they had made up a song to roll cotton by:

"Jine dat coonjine, roll dat bale!
Jine dat coonjine, down de hill!
Gimme little coonjine, coonjine, coonjine,
Gimme little coonjine, please ma'am.
Ain't had none in a long time!"

So with John Henry toting and all the other niggers rolling, and everybody coonjining and singing, the *Big Jim White* loaded on ten thousand bales of cotton that day and dragged it every bit down the river.

"Biggest load of cotton we ever dragged," said the mate.

"Cotton-rollinest niggers I ever drive," said the driver. " 'Cause dey learnt how to coonjine from old John Henry, dat coonjinin' fool!"

THE BLACK RIVER COUNTRY

Hog meat was high. Too high for the people to eat. They could get all the turnip greens they wanted from the garden. They could lift a head of cabbage at the market, and nobody would mind. And anybody would give them a handful of whippoorwill peas. But who can eat turnip greens without a piece of middlin' meat to cook them down with? What good is a head of cabbage if you haven't got a ham shank to boil along in the pot? And a dog wouldn't eat whippoorwill peas that wasn't simmered with a hog jowl, let alone a man.

So the old captain of the *Big Jim White* heard the news, and he decided that the people ought to have a heap of hogs. But he didn't know what to do about it, so he asked the mate. And the mate didn't know, so he asked the driver.

"Hit's a rousterbout named John Henry," said the driver, "which go about singin' a hog song. But I can't tell what he means."

So they sent for John Henry and told him to sing his hog song. So he sang it:

> "Hog-eye gal name Lulu Bell,
> Hog-eye gal name Mabel.
> Hair on her haid like a hoss's mane,
> And mouf as big as a table."

"Where'd you come from, John Henry?" said the captain.

"I comed f'm de Black River country whar de sun don't never shine," said John Henry.

"Whar all de good rousterbouts comes f'm," said the mate.

"Any hogs in the Black River country?" said the captain.

"Must be," said John Henry, "or else how come me singin' dat hog song?"

So the captain turned to the mate and said, "Hoist your stage, you mate!" And he turned to the pilot and said, "Blow your whistle, you pilot!" And he turned to the engineer and said,

"'Twist her tail, you engineer! 'Cause we're going hog-hauling so the people can eat! We're going to the Black River country where the sun don't never shine!"

Hogs run wild in the Black River country. Wild and tall. When the Black River people want a side of middlin' or a ham shank or a jowl, they set their dogs in the woods and the dogs run the hogs into a pen. Sometimes the people kill the tall, wild hogs, and sometimes the tall, wild hogs kill the people. If the people kill the hogs they have meat. If the hogs kill the people, they don't need any meat. It is the way they do in the Black River country where the hogs grow high and wild, with razor-sharp backs and tusks like a knitting-needle. They are bad hogs, but they make good meat.

So the captain landed the *Big Jim White* in the Black River country and asked the people if they had any hogs.

"No hogs," said the Black River people. "But we've got dogs and pens and the woods is full of hogs."

"Can't the dogs run the hogs on the steamboat?" asked the mate.

"No," said the people. "They run the hogs into the pens. It is the best our dogs will do."

"We might build a runway from the pens to the boat," said the captain, "but who is going to run the hogs down the runway?"

"Put de hogs in de pen," said the driver. "Since I been de he-coon on de *Big Jim White,* I ain't never seed nothin' yit my rousters couldn't roust efn they kin git they hands on hit."

So the dogs ran the hogs into the pen. "There they are," said the Black River people. "In a pen six feet tall. It's the best our dogs will do."

"Dat's aplenty," said the driver. "Now ev'y-body jest stand back and gimme plenty room."

So everybody stood back, and the driver stood up tall and bellered: "Come on, you rousters! Gimme dem hogs! We been hyar too long now, and we ain't gone yit! Gimme dem hogs on de *Big Jim White,* so's we kin shake our tail on down de line! Hit dat plank, you bullies, and load dis steamboat down! 'Cause I'm de old he-coon on de *Big Jim White,* and I'm shoutin' workin' news!"

Well, when the rousters heard the driver beller and bawl like that, they swarmed around the hog-pen like flies in molasses.

One rouster got an ear of corn and tried to toll a big hog down to the boat. But as soon as the big hog got clear of the pen he made a break for the big woods. "Good-by, hog," said the rousterbout. "Go find yo' new-found home."

Another rouster grabbed a hog by the hind leg and tried to drag him on the boat. But the big Black River hog kicked just one time, and he kicked that rousterbout from the hog-pen clear to the main deck! "Dat ain't no hog," said the rouster. "Dat's a mule. Or else he got mule blood in his heart."

So another rouster grabbed a hog by the ear, but the hog slobbered and whetted his tusks and all at once he reached up and nearly bit the poor boy's arm off! "Whyn't I stay in de sawmill?" said the poor rouster. "I thought a band saw was bad. But dis hog done ruint me sho'!"

"Gimme dem hogs, you bullies," yelled the driver. "We been hyar too long and we can't stay all day. Grab dem hogs and trot along. What kind er rousters is y'all niggers? Gimme dem hogs and le's git goin'! 'Cause business is better down de line!"

"Hold on," said the captain. "Them niggers can't handle them tall, wild hogs!"

"A good rouster," said the driver, "is jue' to handle anything he kin git his hands on. But dem niggers ain't good rousters. Dey had ought to be plowin' cotton right now."

"I wisht I was," said the rouster that got kicked.

"Or else," said the one that got bit, "I wisht I was settin' blocks in a mean old sawmill some-whar."

"John Henry," said the driver, "what do you wisht you was doin'? You's f'm de Black River country whar de good rousterbouts come f'm, so tell me what you wisht you was doin'."

"Me," said John Henry, "I wisht I was gittin' around. But hit ain't no way to git around to all dese hogs is on de boat. So stand back, you babies, and watch old John Henry roust dese hogs. I'm f'm de Black River country whar de sun don't never shine! So stand back, you field hands, whilst I rousts dese hogs outn de pen! Line up, you bullies, and make yo' shoulders bare! 'Cause when I h'ists dese hogs outn de pen, you gonter think hit's rainin' hogs on yo' weary back. Line up, you clodhoppers and git ready to wawk away. 'Cause my name is John Henry and I'm six foot tall!"

Then John Henry quit his big-talk and circled the pen seven times. Then he got down on his all-fours and circled it seven times more. Then he crept into the pen and lay down on the ground.

"Look like a big boar shote," said a rouster-bout.

"Don't make no fuss," said John Henry, " 'cause I'm handlin' dese hogs. You fight a hog and he fight back. You friend a hog and he friend back. So line up, you bullies, and git yo' shoulders bare!"

So John Henry eased along on his all-fours until he got to the biggest boar shote in the pen.

"Oonk!" said John Henry to the boar shote.

"Oonk! Oonk!" said the boar shote to John Henry.

"Oomp!" said John Henry.

"Oomp! Oomp!" said the boar shote.

"Well, dat's de way I likes to hyar a hog tawk to John Henry," he said. And before that big boar shote knew what was happening, John Henry had done flipped him flat on his back and hoisted him over the pen and on the shoulders of a big rousterbout named Sam! "Now, grab

[19]

him and wawk!" said John Henry. "Tote him like a sack er meal!"

The rouster named Sam walked, and another and another, until the first thing anybody knew there were a hundred rousters walking up and down the plank, toting those big, wild Black River hogs on their shoulders! And before sundown there were ten thousand hogs on the *Big Jim White!*

"I'm loaded down," said the captain, "so hoist your plank, you mate, and blow your whistle, you pilot, and pull her tail, you engineer. We'll take these hogs down the line so the people can eat."

"And all on account er big John Henry," said the driver. "He got his hands on dem Black River hogs, and he rousted 'em down de line. And dat makes him a good rouster 'cause he's f'm de Black River country whar all de good rousters come f'm."

"I'm f'm de Black River country," said John Henry, "and I kin roust what I kin git my hands on. But dat don't make me no rouster. I'm f'm de Black River country whar de sun don't never shine. My home ain't hyar, and I'm fixin' to git around.

THE BLACK RIVER COUNTRY

"So h'ist dat plank, you bullies,
    And mash dat whistle down!
So pull her tail, you engineer,
    And watch me git around!"

BEND YOUR BACK AND SING

IT WAS the year of the big cotton crop when the price was low that John Henry came to the Bends. The stalks were high and white and the fields looked like snow on the mountain-top. The whiter the fields got the more niggers the boss man sent to the field and the more niggers the boss man sent to the field the whiter the fields got.

"If you niggers don't pick this cotton out," the boss man told them, "it will drop out of the bolls and rot on the ground. Come on, you niggers! Snatch that cotton and sack it. It's not worth but eleven cents a pound and we need every lock of it! Pick cotton, black folks! Pick white cotton!"

"Pickin' all de time, Cap'm; you jest can't see me," said the niggers. And they leaned against the cotton like a breeze in the tree.

But the field stayed white and the sacks wouldn't fill.

"I picks to my fingers bleeds at de knuckles," said a cotton-picking man. "I works to my back aches like a pain. But I jest can't git dis cotton picked out clean."

"De bolls bust open right in my face," said another man, "and de locks drop out and rot on de ground. But I'm workin' as hard as I kin."

"Never mind the talking," said the boss man. "Your job is to pick. Cotton don't bring but eleven cents, and it's dropping all the time. If we don't get eleven cents for every lock of this cotton we can't pay out this fall. If it goes to ten cents before we get it picked out, we'll all go to the poorhouse. Now come on, you niggers! Snatch it, and snatch it clean! You can't hardly sell clean cotton, let alone all the bolls and stalks you're grabbing. Bend your backs and snatch cotton!"

So the niggers bent their backs and snatched hard, but the cotton hung to the bolls and wouldn't come out clean.

The boss man watched them bend their backs and snatch cotton, and he saw he wasn't getting anywhere. So he said:

"Throw down, you niggers! Throw down your sacks, because we can't get this cotton out this fall, and we can't pay out. So throw down your sacks and line up. We'll turn the cows in this cotton, and give the field to the sheriff, and we'll all go marching up to the poorhouse door! So throw down your sacks, you bullies, and line up!"

"Wait a minute, Cap'm!" It was John Henry, and he was six feet tall the day he said it. "Cows don't want dis cotton and de sheriff don't want dis land. Eleven-cent cotton will pay us out, but hit won't he'p de cows. And de sheriff ain't gonter git no good outn dis field."

"Neither is anybody else," said the boss man. "The cotton is dropping and the niggers can't keep up. They bend their backs and work hard as they can and don't get nowhere; I'm going to make them throw down and quit. I won't drive my niggers. So get your bundle, boy, and line up for the poorhouse. Because we can't pay out this fall."

"Dat's de trouble, Cap'm," said John Henry.

BEND YOUR BACK AND SING

"Dem niggers is workin' but dey ain't pickin' cotton. Hit's all right to work when hit's work to be done, but when hit's cotton to be picked, well, you ought to forgit de work and go to pickin'."

"Big boy," said a field hand, "efn you don't think cotton-pickin' is work, well, jest bend yo' back and snatch. Look at my poor hands whar de bolls gnawed down to de bone! I snatches white cotton outn de bolls, but befo' I gits hit in de sack hit's turned red wid de blood from my poor knuckles. And when you do like dat, John Henry, well, dat's pyore work."

So John Henry stood up straight and laughed. "Listen at me, you bullies," he said. "Listen at John Henry show you somethin' which don't nobody but me know, and I'll show you how to pick cotton."

So John Henry got him a sack and swung it to his left shoulder, and he got another sack and swung it to his right shoulder.

"Now, line up, you niggers and watch me," he said. "Line up and watch John Henry."

So all the niggers lined up and John Henry showed them.

"Hold yo' fingers a little bent and let yo' hands

[25]

pass by de bolls. Efn they's nigger blood in yo' fingers de cotton will stick and follow. But you won't be gittin' nowheres."

And he passed his hands over the bolls and the cotton followed his fingers, but it fell to the ground.

"You got to cup yo' hands to ketch hit, and move twarge de sack, all de same time," he said. "Not fast; jest slow and stiddy." And he showed them how.

"But efn you straighten up and bend over, ev'y time you picks a boll," John Henry told them, "you' back will weary you down. So you got to bend yo' back and keep hit bent." And he showed them that, too, and the cotton fairly jumped from the bolls and rode his hands to the sack.

"Now you niggers git at dis cotton like I showed you," he said, "and we'll all pay out dis fall."

So the niggers lined up and went at the cotton. And the locks stuck to their fingers and rode in their hands to the sacks.

"Dis ain't hardly no trouble a-tall," said one cotton-picking man.

"Not at first," said another man, "but efn you

holds yo' back bent so long, hit's gonter git mighty weary. And de more cotton you puts in de sack, well, de harder de sack gonter bear down on yo' shoulder. I know my back gonter git mighty tired befo' all er dis cotton is picked." So he sung himself a little weary song:

"Oh, my back hit hurt me so bad, darlin',
'Cause dis cotton bears down so hard on me ——"

"And dat's de trouble," said John Henry. "You niggers is pickin' weary cotton, and you'll be burnt out in no time. 'Cause hit's hard enough to pick cotton wid yo' hands. But when you starts pickin' wid yo' hands and yo' minds bofe, well, I couldn't hardly do dat, and I'm John Henry.

"Now, what y'all bullies got to do is pick cotton wid yo' hands and do some yuther somethin' wid yo' minds. Now ev'ybody watch me and jine in de chorus!" So he sang:

"Sell my cotton,
Drink my cawn, 'n'
Haul my ashes
Ev'y mawnin',
'Cause dis ——

JOHN HENRY

"Now, ev'ybody jine in on de chorus," he said,
and they did:

> "Cotton want pickin' so bad,
> Cotton want pickin' so bad,
> Cotton want pickin' so bad—
> O Lawd, what shall I do?"

Well, the niggers got to singing and got their
weary minds off the cotton-picking. And the
first thing anybody knew they had eleven-cent
cotton piled tree-top high at the gin, and everybody paid out that fall!

And all the niggers knew that John Henry
was a man!

ROLL, YOU WHEELERS

J OHN HENRY was getting around during the time when old man Billie Bob Russell was building the Yellow Dog Railroad from Yazoo City through the Delta.

"I'm building me a railroad a thousand miles long," said old man Billie Bob Russell. "I'm buying me a thousand mules and hiring me a thousand niggers, and I'll have me a railroad when the sun goes down."

So he bought the mules and hired the niggers, and then he hired a walking boss.

"Keep my niggers turning, you walking boss," old man Billie Bob Russell said. "A thousand miles is a long piece, and you've got to keep the niggers turning to do it."

"I'll keep 'em turnin'," the walking boss said. "I'll keep 'em turnin' f'm can to can't. I'll drive 'em to de sun goes down. Niggers *and* mules."

"Mind out for my mules," old man Billie Bob Russell said. "A mule costs a hundred dollars, and a nigger is free for the hiring. If a nigger gets too hot, give him his time and hire another. But if a mule gets too hot he gets off his feed and collar galls come on his shoulders. So don't you waste no hundred-dollar mule in that sunshine, you straw boss. You shade my mules when the sun shines hot, and keep my niggers turning."

So that is the way it was when John Henry came to the Yellow Dog Railroad camp. The sun was hot and the mules were in the shade. The niggers were working on the dump, singing that water-roo song:

"Water-roo, water-roo, bring yo' water 'round.
Efn you ain't got no water, set yo' bucket down!"

The niggers had been on that dump since before sunup and they wouldn't get to leave until the sun went down. But the dump was too short and not high enough to build the Yellow Dog Railroad on. And although there were a thousand niggers in the sun and a thousand mules in the shade, the Yellow Dog Railroad wasn't started!

ROLL, YOU WHEELERS

So John Henry went to the shade and looked at the mules. They were skinny and off their feed. He pulled up their collars and saw big heat galls on their shoulders. And then he went to the mule-pen to catch himself a team of mules.

"How come hit ain't no mule wid his shoulder well?" John Henry asked the stable boss. " 'Cause when I drives a wheeler I got to have a big team or mules wid they shoulders well. Or else I might git mad and drag dat big roller myse'f!"

The stable boss didn't say a word. He just lay back on a bale of hay and sang:

"Caught old Blue and I caught old Bell,
  Captain!
Caught old Blue and I caught old Bell,
  Captain!
Caught old Blue and I caught old Bell,
Couldn't find no mule wid his shoulder well,
And I wisht old Billie Bob was in hell—
  Captain!"

"Stop dat singin' about sore-back mules," John Henry told the stable boss. "Stop dat singin' and git me a pair er mules wid they shoulders well. 'Cause I'm John Henry and I'm six foot tall. Git me a black mule which weighs a thousand pounds. And git me a white mule which weigh de same. Git me mules wid jack stripes runnin' f'm they haid to they tail, wid rings around they forelegs and a back band on they withers. Now, git goin', you stable boss, and git me some mules!"

So the stable boss got him a white mule and a black mule with jack stripes from their heads to their tails and rings around their forelegs and a back band on their withers.

"Now, git me some harness, you stable boss," John Henry told him. "Git me some big harness for dis big team er mules. Git second-growth hickory hames, and sweet-iron chains for traces. Git a sawmill belt for a back band, and balin' wire for hame strings. Git me a bridle wid bat-wing blinds, and a bit er twisted crow bars. Git me some lines a hund'ed feet long, and a belly band made outn leather. Make me a double-tree wid a white-oak log, and a single-tree outn hickory. Hitch me to a wheeler wid ten foot-wheels, and a pole like Jacob's ladder. I wants a Johnson bar twenty foot long, and a cypress tree for a breast yoke. So git out er my way, you dirt-eatin' bullies, and watch my wheeler roll!"

Then John Henry rolled out to the dump and

started rolling dirt for old man Billie Bob Russell's Yellow Dog Railroad.

But before he made four rounds the walking boss called him. "Shade dem mules, you big boy," he said. "Shade dem mules f'm dis hot sunshine, and grab you a pick and shovel. Grab dat spade, you dirt-eater, and level down dis fillin'. Somebody told me a nigger could build a railroad track, but hyar we been for a month er Sundays and we ain't hardly got started. One-Eyed Bill Shelly can't run dat Cannon Ball down dis way to we git dis railroad made. So lay hit down level, you dirt-eatin' bullies! Lay dis railroad down!"

So all the niggers laid heavily on their picks and shovels out in the hot sunshine. But they couldn't pass much dirt. So they sang:

> "Look at de sun, hyar de boss man bawl,
> Captain!
> Look at de sun, hyar de boss man bawl,
> Captain!
> Look at de sun, hyar de boss man bawl,
> Don't git paid to way next fall,
> Dat's what he said and dat was all,
> Captain!"

And that was when big John Henry laid his shovel down! And when John Henry laid his shovel down, the ground shook and the walking boss trembled. There were some mighty doings when big John Henry laid his shovel down!

"I'm a man and I don't know my strenk," said big John Henry. "I'm a fool and I don't know my name. But I'm stout like a mule and my name is John Henry, and I laid my shovel down!"

So the walking boss sidled off and picked up a rock. "You look like a man," he said, "and you tawk like a man. But I'm runnin' dis job and I got de say-so. So efn you don't like yo' shovel, well, hyar's yo' time. So git yo' hat, big boy, and lace up yo' travelin' shoes. 'Cause yo' home ain't hyar!"

"You might be right," said John Henry, "and you might be wrong. But befo' you gimme my time, you better ax Mister Billie Bob Russell!"

"I'm right," said the walking boss. "Mister Billie Bob said to shade de mules and keep de niggers turnin'. And you ain't turnin' wid yo' shovel down."

"Yeah," said John Henry, "and he told you to build a railroad a thousand miles long. But you ain't hardly started."

"I keep de niggers turnin'," said the walking

boss, "and I keep de mules shaded f'm de hot sunshine. Maybe Mister Billie Bob buildin' de railroad. I don't know. Do de road git built or don't she, hit's all one and de same. I keep de niggers turnin' and I keep de mules shaded."

"What's the matter here?" It was old man Billie Bob Russell himself, and he was toting a forty-four gun on each hip. "How am I going to get a thousand miles of railroad built with my walking boss arguing all the time with my niggers? You've been here a month of Sundays, and this road ain't started. What's the trouble, you walking boss? Are you getting tired? Do you want your time?"

"Naw, suh," said the walking boss. "I'm keepin' de niggers turnin' and I'm keepin' de mules shaded. But I ain't gittin' nowhars wid de railroad line."

"Hit ain't none er mine," said John Henry, "but I kin tell you why. You's drivin' niggers. Dat's why. You kin build a railroad or you kin drive niggers. But you can't do bofe at once."

"You know how to build a railroad?" old Billie Bob asked.

"My name is John Henry," he told old Billie Bob, "and I ain't never built a railroad yit. But ain't nobody else ever built one onless dey worked both de niggers *and* de mules."

"Talk on," said Billie Bob Russell. "Let's hear your say."

"You's shadin' de mules in de shade," said John Henry, "and you's drivin' de niggers in de sun."

"Sun don't hurt niggers," said Billie Bob Russell.

"And neither mules," said John Henry. "But you got de mules in de shade, and look at 'em. Dey's skinny like a snake 'cause dey's offn they feed, and hit ain't hardly none wid they shoulder well."

"That's a fact," said Billie Bob Russell. "But mules cost too much money to put in the sun, when the shade won't do them any good."

"Shade," said John Henry, "is made for white fo'ks and hosses. Sun is made for mules and niggers. But don't drive 'em. Drivin' make a nigger weary, and a weary nigger make a mule fall offn his feed, jes to look at 'em. So efn you wants to git dis Yaller Dog built, Mister Billie Bob Russell," said John Henry, "you give yo' wawkin' boss his time and give yo' niggers two big mules and a wheeler. And den you lay back in de shade and watch dis railroad grow!"

ROLL, YOU WHEELERS

"Go to it," said Billie Bob Russell. "Go to it, you niggers, and build my railroad line. Because John Henry is a railroading man and his wheeler's got ten-foot wheels!"

So they built the Yellow Dog Railroad before the sun went down, but John Henry wasn't there when the job was done. For John Henry was a man and he meant to get around!

BACK OF TOWN

I T WAS early one rainy morning when John
Henry got to New Orleans. He came walking in on the hundred-foot stage of the *Big Jim
White,* and the *Big Jim White* pulled in in style.
Her whistle was blowing and her bell was ringing
and her big side wheels were pitching water a
hundred feet high.

"Don't mind me," John Henry said, and he
pranced up and down that hundred-foot stage.
"Don't pay me no mind 'cause I got laigs like a
man and I wawks about."

And before the *Big Jim White* touched the
landing John Henry stepped off the stage and on
top of the freight shed, and that big man from
the Black River country kept right on walking.

BACK OF TOWN

He walked up Canal Street with his head held high. "Don't pay me no mind," he said, " 'cause I'm six foot tall and I'm gittin' around. My name is John Henry f'm I don't know whar."

"Yo' name is John Who-ry?" a nigger named Sam asked him.

John Henry looked at Sam and he looked at himself. Sam was dressed up in a box coat and peg-top pants, with bright yellow shoes and a necktie that made you blind to look at it.

"My name," he said, "is John Henry. I comes f'm de Black River country whar de sun don't never shine. Dat's how come I got on overhalls and jumper. And I'm gittin' around and dat's how come I stepped offn de *Big Jim White*."

So the nigger named Sam looked at John Henry and then he looked up and down the street. "Whar you gittin' around to, John Henry?" he asked him. "You's in town right now. So whar you gittin' around to?"

John Henry didn't say a word. He just opened his mouth and sang a song:

"I been to de east and I been to de west,
  And I reckon I been all around.
I been on de river on de *Big Jim White*,

[39]

So I'm huntin' for de back er town, Lawd, Lawd,
And I'm huntin' for de back er town."

When Sam heard that he laughed. "Fast nigger, hunh?" he asked John Henry.

"Nawp," said John Henry. "Jest big and playful. I been workin' so hard, and now I'm fixin'
to play."

So Sam didn't say a word. He opened his
mouth and sang the John Hardy song back at
John Henry:

"John Hardy he went to de gamblin'-house;
He didn't had no money for to spend.
Long come Poor Selma wid a dollar in her hand,
Say, leave John Hardy in de game, Lawd, Lawd,
Say, leave John Hardy in de game."

And when he finished that song he got up
and told John Henry, he said, "You follow along
behind me."

Sam led John Henry down to Saratoga Street
and into a gambling-house.

"John Henry," he said, "I want you to meet
up wid my friend, John Hardy. John Hardy,"
he said, "John Henry been workin' so hard, and
he want to play. He comed f'm de Black River
country whar de sun don't never shine." And

then he whispered into John Hardy's ear: "He's a country nigger come to town on de excursion. Look at dem clothes he wearin' and you kin tell he a country nigger come to town."

"Sho, John Henry," said John Hardy. "I been hyarin' about you. Somebody told me you was kind er handy wid de cyards. Or was hit de dices? Maybe you'd like to play a little seven-up?"

"Four-up," said John Henry. " 'Cause seven-up takes jest dat much longer." And he sat down to the table with John Hardy, that gambling-man, and the women came and stood behind his chair and sang a song to make him feel lucky so he would bet:

> "I bet he a gamblin', gamblin'-man,
>   And he gamble all around.
>   Ev'ytime he sees him a deck er cyards
>   He th'ows his money down, Lawd, Lawd.
>   And he th'ows his money down."

"I ain't no gamblin'-man," said John Henry, "but I'm gonter set hyar and mock a gamblin'-man!" And he laid a solid silver dollar on the table!

"Fade me, John Hardy," John Henry said. "Four-up ain't my game, but I plays hit for a dollar. Four-up, coon-can, skin, or dices. Hit's all one and de same to me, and I plays you even."

So John Hardy, that gambling-man, he dealt the cards and he went out on John Henry on the first hand.

"Got another dollar, country boy?" he asked. "Lay another dollar on de table and den name de game you wants to play."

So John Henry laughed and laid *two* dollars on the table! "Hit's all one and de same to me," he said. "Only hit's my deal dis time."

John Henry took the cards and dealt, and he turned a jack.

"You deals right good for a country boy," said John Hardy. "Maybe you's a gamblin'-man dressed up like a country boy."

"Maybe," said John Henry, "and maybe not. But I kin see a jack on de turn and I kin see high, low, and de game in my hand, and I'm out on my deal. So I don't want no change, you gamblin'-man. Hit's four dollars on de table, and I can't pick up no change."

"Hit's my deal," said John Hardy.

"Hit is," said John Henry, and he stood up and pulled off his jumper. "Yeah, hit sho is yo' deal," he said, and he stood up and pulled off his

undershirt. And when he did that John Hardy
saw the big arms and shoulders on that big man
from the Black River country where the sun
don't never shine. "I'm too stout," said John
Henry, "to set hyar argyin' about who deal hit
is. What I'm argyin' about is, anybody which
deals had better deal 'em straight."

So when John Hardy saw the big muscles and
the mean look on that big man from the Black
River country, he looked at Sam. And Sam
looked at John Hardy. Then they both looked
out the window. And about that time the
women who were watching the two gambling-
men started singing:

"He laid down de ace and he laid down de king,
   He laid de boss cyards down all around.
He laid down de jack and he laid down de deuce,
   So dey laid him in de buryin'-ground, Lawd, Lawd,
   And dey laid him in de buryin'-ground."

Then John Henry stood up and jumped on
top of the table. "John Hardy," he said, "I didn't
seed you pa'm no cyards, and you didn't see me
pa'm no cyards. And we bofe went out on our
deals. So dat makes us even."

"I didn't know you was a gamblin'-man," said

[43]

John Hardy. "Me my name is old High-Low-Jack-and-de-Game John Hardy, and I th'ows my money away. But Sam told me you was a country nigger wid more wages den brains. So when you turned dat jack on yo' deal, I thought hit was luck, and when you made high, low, and de game and out, I thought you lucked out. But now you's tawkin' like a gamblin'-man, and hit ain't no need in us gamblin' ag'in' each other, 'cause we plays even. And I don't need yo' money and you don't want mine. So what you say, John Henry? Le's be friends, me and you? What you say?"

"I ain't no gamblin'-man," said John Henry, "but I kin mock de man which is." And he reached down and picked up the four dollars that were on the table.

"Money," said John Henry, "ain't no good to me, so I'm gonter give dis money away." And he handed the money to Sam.

"Hyar, Sam," he said, "you kin have dis four dollars 'cause I don't need no money. I don't need no money 'cause when a man is dressed up he don't need no money, and I'm fixin' to git dressed up, so's I kin git around dis town in style.

"So take dis four dollars, Sam, and go buy me

a four-dollar Stutson hat, and I don't want no change back. And you go buy me a bright new suit er clothes wid a box coat and peg-top pants, wid pearl buttons on de pockets and braid around de collar. You buy me some bright yaller shoes, and de reddest socks you kin find. I wants a necktie which makes me blind, and a four-inch standing collar. You buy me dat stuff, Sam," John Henry told him, "and don't bring me back no change. Buy me a big gold watch and a diamond ring, and a horseshoe pin for my necktie. Buy me a gallon jug of sweet perfume and a solid silver toothpick. 'Cause I'm John Henry and I'm six foot tall, and I aims to git around some. So gang around, you bullies, and listen at John Henry. Y'all ladies been standin' behind me, dig down in yo' stockin's. 'Cause Sam gonter need him a heap er cash to git me all dressed up. Dig down, you gamblers! Dig down deep, and spend yo' gamblin'-money. 'Cause I'm big John Henry f'm I don't know whar and I'm fixin' to git around some."

So all the women dug down in their socks and John Hardy dug down in his pockets, and the first thing anybody knew, Sam had his hat full of money.

[45]

JOHN HENRY

"Now come on, Sam," said John Henry, "and we go buys de store out. 'Cause I'm gonter dress like a dead-game sport, so all y'all gals and gamblers won't jump on a poor country boy when he is big and playful. So come on, Sam, and bring dat change, 'cause I'm big John Henry!"

JULIE ANNE

W HEN John Henry started getting around in New Orleans he went out and got himself all dressed up. His suit was the stripedest one in the stores. His socks were the reddest ones he could find. And his shoes were muddy brown. His shirt was so blue it looked like the sky, and his hat was on the back of his head. He had a gold watch and a horseshoe pin, and his tie made people go sit on the corner with a tin cup begging because they were blind. His coat was square like a drygoods box and his pants pegged out like an umbrella.

"Stand back, y'all ladies," John Henry said, "so's ev'ybody kin see me. Don't come swarmin' around too close, 'cause I needs plenty er room."

So about that time there was a girl named

JOHN HENRY

Ruby came up to John Henry and said, "Hello, Big Stuff! Whar you goin' all by yo' lonesome?"

And before John Henry could say a word to her, a girl named Delia came up and took John Henry by the arm. "Dis big bully ain't lonesome," she said, "so long as his Delia gal is around. Is you, Big'n'?"

So John Henry looked at Ruby and he looked at Delia. Then he looked up and down the street. And when he looked up and down the street he saw a woman named Julie Anne. She looked at John Henry and then she looked at Ruby and Delia, but she didn't say a silent word. She sang:

> "John Henry was so big and tall,
>   I reckon he was a man,
>   He comed to de city and he got dressed up,
>   And he seed poor Julie Anne, Lawd, Lawd,
>   Den he seed poor Julie Anne."

"How come you know I'm John Henry?" he asked her.

"You's six foot tall," said Julie Anne, "and you's gittin' around, ain't you?"

"Sho I'm six foot tall," said John Henry, "and I'm gittin' around. But hit's a heap er niggers six foot tall and gittin' around. I seed a nigger named Sam which is six foot tall and gittin' around."

"Look at me, John Henry," said Julie Anne. "I's six foot tall, too. And I got blue gums and gray eyes."

"I got blue gums and gray eyes, too," said John Henry. "But dat don't make me John Henry, do hit? Let alone, you?"

"And," said Julie Anne, "I comed f'm de Black River country whar de sun don't never shine."

"Me too," said John Henry, "and my name is John Henry, but dat don't make me yo' man."

"Well," said Julie Anne, "I ain't argyin' wid you, John Henry. But don't you forgit, you's my man. 'Cause they's a *gris gris* on me and you."

"I'm a man," said John Henry, "and I'm six foot tall. But I'm my own."

"You's my man, John Henry," said Julie Anne. And she went in the house and shut the door.

So John Henry walked on down the street where Ruby was. "She's crazy," he said, and he took Ruby by the right hand.

"Sing me a song, Sweet Thing," he said, " 'cause I likes de way you sing."

Ruby laughed and backed off. "Aw, you don't know," she said. "You ain't never hyared me sing."

"Well," said John Henry, "I likes de way you opens up yo' mouf. So come and sing at me."

"Nunh-unh," said Ruby. "You jest funnin' wid me."

"Aw, come on and please sing at me," said John Henry.

"Please ain't gittin' me nothin', you great big old dead-game spo't," Ruby told him. "I might sing at you and you might squeeze de stuffin' outn me 'cause you'd like me so good."

So John Henry he stood and begged her awhile, and Ruby she kept arguing and putting him off, and laughing and trying to draw him on. And the more she would put John Henry off the more he would beg her to sing for him. Until, finally, John Henry got tired of it.

"Now, gal," he said, "I'm fixin' to ax you one more time. Is you gonter sing for me or ain't you?"

"How come I got to sing for you, Big'n'?"

Ruby asked him. "You great big old man jest vexes a gal like me ——"

"You ain't," said John Henry. "You jest want me to beg you, and I'm tired er beggin'. So goodby, Ruby, and good-by, all. 'Cause I don't like you no more." And he walked off.

"Wait, John Henry," said Ruby. "I'm fixin' to sing for you. I was jest playin', John Henry, darlin'. I was aimin' to sing for you all de time. I was jest funnin'."

"No mind," said John Henry. "I don't want to hyar you sing."

"But I got a good song, John Henry," Ruby told him, and she tried to grab John Henry by the right hand. But he shoved her away.

"Git away, gal," he told her. "Go play wid somebody which got time and patience. Me, I'm f'm de Black River country, and I don't know what time is." And he walked away from Ruby.

"Ruby is a fool," Delia told John Henry, and she took him by the right hand. " 'Cause when a big man like you wants a gal to sing for him, well, he don't want her to ack like she was a kitten, do he? But me, darlin', I know how a big man like you want a gal to ack. I'm gonter sing you a song widout you axin' me." So she sang:

JOHN HENRY

"He looked at de sky and he looked at de ground,
    Jest to see what he could see,
And he couldn't see nothin' but his Delia gal,
    And Delia had a stinger-ree, Lawd, Lawd,
    Poor Delia had a stinger-ree."

John Henry listened to her song and when she got done he shook his head. "Well," he said, "I reckon I'll be gittin' around." And he walked off.

"Wait a minute, John Henry," Delia told him. "Didn't I sing purty for you?"

"Sho you sung purty for me," said John Henry. "But now you done sung yo' song. So hit ain't no need to stand hyar and argy about hit."

"You want me to sing some more?"

"Nawp," said John Henry. "Once is aplenty."

"I kin sing another song more gooder den dat'n'," said Delia.

"Sing yo' song to some yuther man which ain't sick and tired er singin'," said John Henry.

"But you likes singin', and I likes to sing," said Delia.

"You's too anxious," said John Henry. "Ruby she wasn't anxious enough, and now you's too anxious. Ruby she was plenty er trouble, but you's a heap worse. So gimme my hat, you Delia gal, and watch old John Henry ramble."

So John Henry left Delia and walked up and down the street for a solid mile. He saw a heap of women, but they were all like Ruby or Delia. Some of them weren't anxious enough to please him, and some of them were too anxious. So finally he came back and knocked on the door.

"Come on in, John Henry," Julie Anne told him. "I been waitin' for you to come back."

"How'd you know I'm John Henry," he asked her, "and how'd you know I was comin' back?"

"You's John Henry," said Julie Anne, "and you's back. So no mind how I knowed. I jest knowed hit all de time, and no mind how."

"Well," said John Henry "s'posin' I gits up and leaves right now? You know anything like dat?"

"John Henry," said Julie Anne, "you's a natchal man and you come and go when you please. And when and whar, hit ain't none er mine. Only, when you gits tired er trampin' round de streets you gonter come back to yo' Julie Anne."

"Looky hyar, gal," said John Henry, "you think you got a stinger-ree on me? You think I can't quit you and stay quit? You think yo' name is Poor Selma?"

"Nawp," said Julie Anne. "I ain't got no stinger-ree, and you kin quit me like quittin' work. And I ain't no Poor Selma, and I ain't tryin' to hold you down. But look at dis, John Henry," and she opened her mouth and pointed to her blue gums. "And look at dis," and she opened her eyes and pointed to her gray eyeballs. "Hit ain't no stinger-ree and hit ain't no Poor Selma. Hit's just de way hit is. Hit's on you de same as on me. Hit's a *gris gris* on you and on me. Hit's de way things is, John Henry. I didn't put hit dar, no more'n you. But dar hit is.

"So when you feel like goin', John Henry," she told him, "jest git yo' hat and git yo'se'f on down de road. And when you feel like comin' back, jest wawk in and th'ow you' shoes under de bed and stay to yo' heel start eetchin' to travel some more. 'Cause you'll stay awhile and you'll ramble awhile. But you'll always come back to yo' Julie Anne, 'cause I'm yo' woman and you's my man, and hit ain't no he'p fer dat."

So big John Henry put his shoes under the bed and took Julie Anne by the right hand. "You sing me a song, gal," he told her.

JULIE ANNE

"I'll sing you a song," Julie Anne said, "but you got to sing bass for me."

"All right," said John Henry. "You sing and I'll bass."

So she sang:

"John Henry had him a purty little gal
    And her name was Julie Anne.
He knowed she was his lovin' wife
    And he was her lovin' man, Lawd, Lawd,
    And dey bofe went hand-in-hand."

FOURTEEN-THIRTY-SIX

THE sun was shining hot the day John Henry made up his mind to quit laying around. He had been laying around back of town for a long time with his fancy clothes and he was having a heap of fun. But he got tired of it and decided to get him a job of work. " 'Cause dis kind er way might be all o. k. for dem which likes hit," he said, "but hit ain't no way for a man."

"Hit ain't no need in you goin' to work, John Henry," Julie Anne told him. "I got a job and hit ain't no need in me and you bofe workin'. So long as hit's a nickel in my sock, darlin', you ain't 'bliged to turn yo' hand."

"Git me my overhalls, woman," John Henry told her. "Git me my overhalls and my jumper. 'Cause dis layin' around is killin' me sho."

FOURTEEN-THIRTY-SIX

"You looks a heap sweeter in dem fancy clothes," Julie Anne told him, "but efn you's bound to work, well, don't let me stop you. 'Cause you's a man, John Henry, and you knows yo' mind."

So John Henry put on his overalls and his jumper and went out where the white folks had all the niggers working on the streets. He stood around and watched the niggers dig down in the ground, and he watched the swing of their picks and shovels to the tune they were singing:

> "Ef-er you don't think I'm sinkin'—wham!
> Lawd, looky what a hole I'm in—wham!"

About that time the cap'm saw John Henry standing around. So he said, "Boy, what are you hanging around here for?"

"I'm huntin' me a job er work," said John Henry. "I'm a man and I'm tired er layin' around, so I'm huntin' a job er work."

"You just hang around," the cap'm told him, "and you'll get all the work you want." And he turned his back on John Henry and started driving the niggers. "Lay on it, you gobblers," he told them. "Bear down on them handles and let me see a hole in the ground! Hump it up, you bullies, or there's worse than this in the parish!"

So all the niggers made a terrible fuss like they were working faster, and they sang a new song. One man said:

"Poor Selma was my stinger-ree gal;
　　She swore she'd go my bail,
But de Law said, Fourteen-thirty-six,
　　And dey laid me in de parish jail, Lawd, Lawd,
　　And dey laid me in de parish jail."

Everybody laughed at that song, and another man sang:

"Ruby she lived on Franklin Street
　　Right whar I had me a home,
But along comes a bully in a big box coat,
　　And now I'm bustin' stones, Lawd, Lawd,
　　Got me breakin' up de rocks and stones."

Then another man sang:

"Poor Delia she was my happy gal,
　　Twice as happy as she could be.
But she tuck to gin and she tuck to coke,
　　And now take a look at me, Lawd, Lawd,
　　Jest take a look at poor me."

FOURTEEN-THIRTY-SIX

But when the next man sang, everybody did laugh:

> "You lay yo' sorrows to a woman's name,
>   And yo' burdens to a woman's ways,
> But I'm gonter tell you how come I'm hyar,
>   'Cause de judge said, Sixty days, Lawd, Lawd,
>   Judge Leonard said, Sixty days."

John Henry listened to the singing as long as he could stand it, and when he couldn't stand it any longer, he stood up and sang his song:

> "Sing about yo' woman, well, you ain't seed mine.
>   And her name is Julie Anne.
> She tell me, Darlin', ef I got one dime
>   You ain't got to turn yo' hand, Lawd, Lawd,
>   You ain't got to turn yo' hand."

So when John Henry started singing the big old cap'm turned around and looked at him.

"You still hanging around here, boy?" he said.

"I'm huntin' a job er work, Cap'm," John Henry told him.

"All right," said the cap'm. "I'll get you a job!" So he whistled in his fingers like a policeman on his beat, and up walked the Law!

"This boy is hunting a job, Law," the old

cap'm said. "He's been hanging around here all morning. He says as long as his woman has got a dime he don't have to turn his hand."

"Come on, boy," said the Law. "I'll find you a job."

So the Law led John Henry to the First Precinct and locked him in a cage like a bird!

"Dis ain't no work, settin' hyar," said John Henry.

"Sit still," said the Law. "You'll have company pretty soon, for I'm cleaning up Franklin Street."

And sure enough, the first thing John Henry knew, they began filling up the cage with all the people on Franklin Street. John Henry saw the big old nigger named Sam, and John Hardy, the gambler, and Ruby and Delia. And pretty soon he saw Julie Anne!

"Hey, John Henry," said Julie Anne, "you sho is fixin' to git you a job, ain't you?"

"Dat what de Law allow," said John Henry.

"Not so long as I got a dime in my sock, darlin'," she said.

When Ruby heard that she yi-yied at Julie Anne. "When de jedge see a big nigger like him," she said, "de jail ain't big enough to hold him, 'cause dey needs big niggers on de road so bad."

"And," put in Delia, "dey do say de jedge don't know nothin' but 'sixty days,' and dat in de parish! Lawd, Lawd, how long!"

So pretty soon they lined up all the niggers in front of the judge and started to work on them. John Hardy, the gambler, was the first man in line.

"What you got to say, boy?" said the judge.

"I been sick, Jedge," said John Hardy. "I jest got outn de hospital."

"Well," said the judge, "what you need is sunshine. Sixty days on the streets, and you won't feel the same."

So the judge turned to the big nigger named Sam. "What you been doin', boy?" he said.

"I been workin'," said Sam, "only I got laid off yistiddy."

"Well, I'm going to lay you on," said the judge. "Sixty days."

So he turned to Ruby. "What have you been doing?" he asked.

"Washin' and ironin' for de white fo'ks," said Ruby.

"But you didn't wash the paint and powder off your own cheeks," said the judge.

"Hit won't wash off," Ruby said.

"Well," said the judge, "I'll put you away in the parish for sixty days, and let's see if it won't wear off."

Then he turned to Delia. "Where you been working?" he said.

"I cooks for de white fo'ks," said Delia.

"Are you a good cook?" said the judge.

"My madam think so," said Delia. "I ain't braggin' ——"

"They need a good cook over at the parish," said the judge. "Sixty days."

And then he looked at John Henry!

"Where you been workin', big boy?" said the judge.

"I ain't been," said John Henry. "I been layin' around for a week. I won some money offn dat boy which say he been sick in de hospital. And dat nigger named Sam he'ped me pick out some fancy clothes. And den I funned around wid de ladies which say dey been washin' and cookin'. And den I and Julie Anne, hyar, tuck up. So I spent all my money, so I put on my overhalls and jumper, and started lookin' around."

FOURTEEN-THIRTY-SIX

"Country nigger, I bet," said the judge.

"I comes f'm de Black River country whar de sun don't never shine," said John Henry.

"Let me see your hands," said the judge. And John Henry held up his hands so the judge could see the work-corns in them.

"Country nigger," said the judge, "you better take your bundle and git. You Black River niggers are too good to stay in this town. These city niggers will take your money and let you starve. They'll steal your woman and laugh in your face. They'll cut your throat and take off your shoes. And they won't even go to your funeral. So get your bundle and get out of town, because this is no place for you."

"I been fixin' to git around some, Cap'm," said John Henry, " 'cause I been hyar too long, now. I worked and den I played. And now I'm fixin' to work some more. So git out er my way, all you Franklin Street niggers. Git out er my way, you bullies, 'cause I'm movin' along. A box coat feel like a coffin on me, and peg pants is pegs in de coffin lid. Yaller shoes might fit some er you rounders' foots, but dey cut too sharp for me. So gimme my overhalls, you Julie Anne. Gimme my overhalls and jumper, 'cause I aims

[63]

to work and play. I done worked and I done played, and now I aims to travel. So farewell, all you Franklin Street bullies. Fare you well, you ladies. 'Cause I'm big and bad and had ought to be chained, and I comes f'm I don't know whar. I'm six foot tall, and I weighs a ton, and my name is writ in my hat!"

WOMAN ON MY WEARY MIND

WHEN John Henry decided to get away from New Orleans he turned his back on the river. He came to New Orleans on the *Big Jim White*, but the old woman told him the *Big Jim White* would never bring him back to the Black River country where he was born.

"Hit carried many a good man down de line," the old woman told him, "but hit ain't never yit brang one back. So mind out, John Henry, and don't roam too far."

It was too far to walk from New Orleans to the Black River country, and John Henry didn't have any wings.

"Snag some old lonesome freight train and ride," Julie Anne told him. "You know what de song say, darlin'. De song say:

JOHN HENRY

"When I git de blues I git de fawty-day blues
    And I can't be satisfied.
Lawd, I gits de blues, I gits de ramblin' blues
    And I can't be satisfied.
So I'm goin' to de depot and snag me a train and ride.

"Dat's what de ramblin' song say, John Henry," she told him. "But hit's still another kind er blues which I'm gonter sing to you:

"He left his purty mamma standin' in de door.
Left his purty mamma, Lawd, a-standin' in de door.
    Hyar's what she told him, darlin',
    Say, you ain't 'bliged to go.

"Dat's another kind er blues, John Henry," she told him. "But you ain't learnt dat song yit, son. You had hit too easy wid de womenfo'ks. So git yo' hat, darlin', and git yo'se'f on down to de depot, John Henry, and you gonter leave me hyar."

So John Henry got his hat and got down to the depot. The big Red Ball freight train, a solid mile long, was just pulling out. He snagged it and climbed on top of a car. "Ramble along, freight train," John Henry said, " 'cause I'm got de Black River country blues and I can't be satisfied."

[66]

WOMAN ON MY WEARY MIND

When the Red Ball got to rattling along over the rails the racket it made put John Henry in mind of the song that Julie Anne had sung to him. So he sang the song the way he felt about it. The air was whipping past his face and the long sugar-cane fields were stretching out like a green blanket. He couldn't smell New Orleans any more, but he could smell the country. Not the Black River country that he was lonesome for, but it was not like talcum powder in New Orleans. So he sang Julie Anne's song his style:

"Left my purty mamma standin' in de door.
Lawd, left my darlin' mamma standin' in de door.
What you reckon I told dat sweet mamma?
Say, I can't use you no more."

But the song didn't satisfy him. He liked the wind in his face and he liked the fresh sweet smell of the country that rolled by. He didn't really want to sing at all, but the clickity-click of the wheels singing against the solid steel rails wouldn't let his mind rest. So he tried another song:

"Let me tell you somethin', let hit bear down on yo' mind.
Listen to me, darlin', let hit bear down on er yo' mind.
'Cause I gits so tired of de same thing all de time."

But that song didn't do him any good, either, and he hollered at the brakeman. "Hey, Mister Brakeman," he said, "I'm ridin' high and I ain't paid no railroad fare. I'm bound for de Black River country whar de sun don't never shine. So kin you please, suh, tell me do dis Red Ball go by dat Black River country, or am I jest ridin' around?"

The brakeman looked at his white-oak brake stick, and then he looked at John Henry. "Big boy," he said, "this Red Ball goes through the Black River country, but it don't slow down. We're due in Memphis before the sun goes down and we ain't hardly got started yet. You see all of them clouds in the east? Well, that is smoke from the engine. You see all that rain in the cane-fields? Well, that's sweat from the fireman's brow. You see all them rocks flying along the cross-ties? Well, that's because the fireman's tongue is dragging the ground.

"Because," said the brakeman, "old man One-eyed Bill Shelly is pulling her tail, and the fireman can't keep up steam."

"Is de fireman got plenty er coal?" John Henry asked him.

"Plenty coal, and water, too," said the brakeman. "But old man One-eyed Bill Shelly is pulling the throttle, and we're due in Memphis before the sun goes down."

"Hit look to me like," said John Henry, "did a good fireman had plenty er coal, and water, too, well, hit look like to me he could keep up de steam."

"This train," said the brakeman, "is a solid mile long and old **man** One-eyed Bill Shelly is twisting her tail."

"I been layin' around," said John Henry, "to I got weary in my mind. So now I'm huntin' me a job er work. Maybe efn dat fireman can't keep up de steam, well, maybe old man One-eyed Bill Shelly would like a fireman which kin."

The brakeman looked at John Henry and he laughed. "Boy," he said, "there's a big nigger named Sam firing that engine. He's the best fireman on the road. That's why he's always firing for old man One-eyed Bill Shelly. So when old Jay Gould told them to put this train in Memphis before the sun goes down, they picked old man Shelly and he picked Sam. And that's how come that bad engineer ain't pulling the throttle on the Cannon Ball today."

"Dis train ain't goin' fast enough to suit me," said John Henry, "let alone old Jay Gould."

"Maybe," said the brakeman, "old man One-eyed Bill Shelly could pull her faster if he could get the steam, and maybe that nigger named Sam could get the steam up if you would push the coal down for him, so what you say, big boy from the Black River country? What do you say to pushing down coal for that fireman named Sam, and let's all get to Memphis before the sun goes down?"

"Maybe," said John Henry, and he went up to the tender to push the coal down. But he just pushed with his foot one time and he pushed all the coal down on that fireman named Sam.

"Mind out, up yonder," said Sam. "You want to bury me wid dis coal? I'm black wid coal, now."

"You was black before dat coal ever tetched you," said John Henry. "Whyn't you git up some steam so's me and Mister One-eyed Bill Shelly kin git dis train to Memphis before de sun goes down?"

"Maybe you think you kin keep up steam for Mister One-eyed Bill Shelly," said Sam. "You niggers runnin' around hyar wid a heap er say-so,

but when hit comes to shovelin' coal for Mister
One-eyed Bill Shelly, I'm de onliest man which
got any do-so, and I can't hardly keep up enough
steam to blow de whistle. And efn you don't
b'lieve dat, how come old Jay Gould picks me
out when he wants to git de train to Memphis
before de sun goes down?"

"Well," said John Henry, "I ain't old Jay
Gould, and I don't keer nothin' about gittin'
to Memphis before de sun goes down. But I do
love to hyar old One-eyed Bill Shelly pull de
highball outn dat whistle. I ain't hyared dat
two longs, a shawt, and a long since I don't know
when. So stand back, you mush-back fireman,
and let old John Henry raise up de steam."

But the fireman looked at John Henry and
laughed. "I fires wid a Number Four shovel,"
he said. "You couldn't hold de firebox door open
for me to fire, let alone keep de coal pourin' in."

"Kin you hold de door open?" asked John
Henry.

"Sho I kin," said the fireman, " 'cause my
name is Sam Rucker, and I'm de best fireman
on old Jay Gould's railroad."

"Gimme de shovel," said John Henry, "and
you hold open de firebox door."

So Sam held open the firebox door and big John Henry took the shovel in his hand.

"Don't git in my way, Sam," said John Henry, " 'cause I'm liable to chunk you in de firebox, and you too greasy to make good steam." And that big man from the Black River country poured a steady stream of coal into the roaring-hot fire and he watched the steam-gauge rise. "Pull her tail, Mister One-eyed Bill Shelly," he said, "and mash dat whistle down, 'cause I'm big and stout and crazy and mean and I don't aim to tetch de ground."

The faster John Henry shoveled, the faster the steam-gauge rose, and the faster the steam-gauge rose the faster old One-eyed Bill Shelly would pull her tail.

Then about that time old One-eyed Bill Shelly told John Henry, he said, "Here's the Black River country where the sun don't never shine."

So John Henry looked out and saw the country rolling by like smoke up the chimney. So he laid on the coal, and then he told old One-eyed Bill Shelly, he said: "Pull her tail, Mister One-eyed Bill, and give her a lonesome high-ball, so all de niggers will lean out de windows and know John Henry went through."

WOMAN ON MY WEARY MIND

Then old One-eyed Bill Shelly whistled the highball and he opened his throttle wide. And that Red Ball freight train was in Memphis before the sun went down.

"John Henry," said One-eyed Bill Shelly, "you fired for me on the Red Ball freight, and you can fire for me on the Cannon Ball. Sam is a good fireman, but he ain't one-two with you. You go walking straight up to old Jay Gould and tell him you're my fireman. Tell him to pay you a dollar a day and give you a Number Four shovel."

But John Henry looked at the shovel and he looked at Memphis. He saw the river and he saw the bluff and he saw the Beale Street women. Then he sat on the high bridge over the river and he sang a song:

"I was bawn on de old Black River
    Whar de sun don't never shine.
  Den I got a runaround on my heels,
  And a woman on my mind, Lawd, Lawd,
    Julie Anne on my weary mind."

POOR SELMA

POOR SELMA was a woman that the men couldn't leave alone. She was tall and rusty and ugly. She had a mean temper and an evil tongue. Her nose was flat and her mouth was big and her lips looked like liver. And when she walked the streets of Argenta the hollow of her foot made a hole in the ground. But she claimed she had a stinger-ree.

Poor Selma had a big white house on the corner of Third and Bird streets. It was a two-story house, with a piano in the parlor and a folding-bed in every room. And the niggers from the Cotton Belt railroad made a path straight to her front door.

"I ain't foolin' wid y'all railroad niggers," Poor Selma told them. "Hit'll cost you money to come to my house, and hit's cost you trouble, too. But you can't stay away, 'cause I'm like de old cocaine habit. I'm bad and I can't be quit. Git you a woman you love and marry her, but bring yo' money to me. Yo' wife might be de four-day fevers, but I'm de wastin' disease. Preachers preach me out on Sunday and den bring de collection box to me. De deacons say I'm a hell-bound sinner, but dey tips dey hat when dey pass me on de street. So sign de pay-roll, you bullies, and lay yo' money down 'cause I'm ugly and I'm mean and don't nobody love me. But de mens can't leave me alone. I lives in a big white two-story house wid a foldin'-bed in ev'y room. So look out, you bullies, 'cause I aims to do you wrong."

So all the Cotton Belt niggers made up a song about Poor Selma that said:

"High-yaller woman make a preacher lay his Bible down.
Brown-skin lady make a deacon turn round and round.
But dat low-down Selma make a mule kick his stable down."

But poor Selma didn't mind how much they sang about her. She didn't have but one song, and she couldn't sing that one very well. But she would sing it in Argenta and then she'd cross

the river and sing it in Little Rock, right in front
of all the married women:

> "Oh, he may be yo' man,
> But he comes to see me sometimes."

That was the way things were around the Cotton Belt shops in Argenta when big John Henry
got to town. John Henry rolled in one night
about eight o'clock on the Cotton Belt from
Memphis. It was a hot night and there were a
heap of clouds in the sky, but no rain to cool
down the air, so John Henry got off the train
and went up the path that led to Poor Selma's
front door at Third and Bird, and he rang Poor
Selma's bell.

"Who dar?" said Poor Selma.

"Don't stand axin' me 'who dar?'" said John
Henry. "Open dat door and let a big man in."

"Railroad nigger?" Poor Selma asked him.

"No mind what kind er nigger I'm is," said
John Henry. "You hyared me ring de bell, didn't
you? Well, den, open up de door."

"Maybe you better not come in," said Poor
Selma. "Maybe you a country nigger and don't
know whar I live at. Maybe you better go on
about yo' business and leave Poor Selma be."

POOR SELMA

So John Henry didn't say a word. He just
opened up his mouth and sang a song at Poor
Selma through the keyhole:

"Well, hit's open up de window
And hit's open up de door,
'Cause my name is John Henry
And I been hyar before,
Hey, hey, honey, take a whiff on me."

"Singin' dat old cocaine song, hunh?" said
Poor Selma. "Well, you know's cocaine, but I'm
worse'n cocaine, 'cause coke won't do nothin'
but kill you. But me? Well, I ain't Poor Selma's
sister and I ain't Poor Selma's mamma, 'cause I'm
dat low-down devil herse'f, and I'm worse'n
cocaine. You kin quit cocaine and den die, but
when you tries to quit me, you can't quit and
den you can't die. Hit's niggers in jail wearin'
de ball and chain which tried to quit me and
couldn't. So mind you out, you John Henry,
'cause I hyars you's a man, and dat's what I'm
after."

"Open up dat door, woman," said John
Henry, "or else I'll git mad and bust hit down."
And when he said that he got mad, so he took
his fist and knocked the door down.

"My woman in New Or-leens don't lock no door on me," said John Henry, "and I don't aim to let you start, 'cause I'm a man and I'm mean and I comes f'm I don't know whar."

"Mind out, darlin'," said Poor Selma. "You tawks like a man and you looks like a man, and you busted my poor door down. Maybe you ain't never hyared er Poor Selma? Maybe you's a country nigger and ain't never been around?"

"Maybe," said John Henry, "and den again, maybe not. When I looks at you I don't see nothin' but a ugly old woman, 'cause you don't look good to me."

Poor Selma laughed when he said that. "Well," she said, "I don't look good and I don't ack good, but, Lawd, Lawd, I got a stinger-ree."

"Lady," said John Henry, "you think you's bad and you can't be quit. I hyared yo' say-so before I come in. But I'm hyar tonight to see is you got any do-so along wid yo' say-so, 'cause I'm big John Henry and I kin quit you like I was quittin' work."

"I quit many a man," said Poor Selma, "but ain't never yit been no man which kin quit me. I does de quittin' in dis house, not you. I ain't much to look at and I ain't much to tawk to,

but I got a *gris gris* on my weary soul. You
wawked in my house er yo' own free mind, but
dat's de last free step you ever gonter take, 'cause
I'm a bad habit and I can't be quit. I'm a hell-
bound sinner, but I knows my name. My name
is Poor Selma and de doctor can't do me no
good."

So big John Henry walked up and took Poor
Selma by the right hand. "Selma," he said, "I'm
a man and I'm six foot tall. I comes f'm de Black
River country whar de sun don't never shine.
But, lady, I'm gittin' around. Now I'm gonter
sing you a song:

"I lived in de country and I lived in de town
    And I'm a toker-loker shaker f'm haid on down.

"Now, you don't know dat song, does you?
'Cause hit's a man's song and you don't know
nothin' about no man yit. You think you's got
a stinger-ree and you think you's a hell-bound
sinner, but you ain't, 'cause de devil don't want
you."

"But you ain't de devil," said Poor Selma.
"You's a man and you's made outn meat, and
dat's all I wants to know about you."

"Well," said John Henry, "you got a heap er

say-so for a ugly old gal like you. But what I wants to know is, is you got any do-so? 'Cause I'm big an bad and got a certain woman on my weary mind."

"Dat's me," said Poor Selma. "You might think hit ain't, but you might jest as well th'ow yo' shoes under de bed and hang yo' hat in de hall, 'cause you might be bad and you might be fast, but Poor Selma gonter wear you down."

"I got a woman on my mind," said John Henry, "but hit sho ain't you. So listen to my weary song, Poor Selma, and see do hit sound familiar:

"I got a gal in New Or-leens,
    And her name is Julie Anne.
She ain't so big and she ain't so black,
    But John Henry is her man, Lawd, Lawd,
    And John Henry is her man.

"Now, Poor Selma," said John Henry, "I been foolin' wid you to I sung you my song. But when I sing my song about a woman in New Or-leens, well, dat de sign you ain't got a thing. I took you by de hand and I th'owed my shoes under yo' bed, and I hung my hat in yo' hall, but all de time I had a woman on my mind, and I never did like yo' looks. You say you's bad like de cocaine habit, and you say you can't be quit. Well, lady, jest watch old John Henry git his shoes and hat and quit you like I'm quittin' work."

Poor Selma looked at John Henry and then she looked at the poor door he broke down with his fist when he came in the house. "Hit's been many a nigger begged to git in," she told him. "And hit's been many a nigger begged to stay. But, John Henry, hit ain't never yit been no man quit poor me. You's tawkin' big, and you's actin' big, but you ain't gone nowhar. So jest th'ow yo' shoes back under de bed, and hang up yo' wawkin'-cane, 'cause old Bad Habit Poor Selma likes you for a man, and she ain't said you kin go."

So John Henry stood up and laughed in Poor Selma's face. Then he put on his shoes and he put on his hat, and he picked up his walking-cane. "Git out er my way, you good little gal, 'cause I aims to git around."

"I ain't said for you to go, darlin'," said Poor Selma. "Ain't no man ever yit ——"

So John Henry didn't say a word. He just opened up his mouth and sang a song that made

[81]

the lightning cleave the air, and the stars burn out like a lamp. Because when John Henry sang his song to Poor Selma it was something no man had ever done before and no man has ever done since. But it was John Henry's song, and he sang it so loud it shook the roof off that big white two-story house at Third and Bird, and it laid Poor Selma down:

> "Poor Selma had her a stinger-ree,
>   Thought she stung John Henry dead.
> But he put on his hat and he put on his shoes,
>   And he wasn't in de foldin'-bed, Lawd, Lawd,
>   Couldn't find him in de foldin'-bed."

And John Henry put on his hat and his shoes and walked right out of Poor Selma's front door like he was walking away from a job of work, because Poor Selma was bad; but John Henry was a man and he was six feet tall, and he came from he didn't know where!

STACKER LEE

I T WAS while John Henry was laying around
in Argenta that he met up with old bad
Stacker Lee. He was walking down Markham
Street in Little Rock when he heard a poor
woman named Ruby singing a song:

> "Stacker Lee was a bad man,
> Twice as bad as he could be.
> Tuck a shot at my poor sister,
> And he tuck a shot at me.
> Ain't he bad, bad Stacker Lee?"

So John Henry walked up to Ruby and said,
"Gal, who dis bad man you singin' about? 'Cause
I ain't named Stacker Lee and I'm de baddest
man in dis town."

The woman looked up and down Markham

JOHN HENRY

Street and then she looked up and down Main. "You wouldn't know efn I told you," she said, "but hyar what de song got to say about him." And she sang again:

"He tuck him a shot er cocaine
And he tuck him a shot er gin,
Den he tuck a shot at his lovin' wife,
And dat's how dis song begins.
Oh, ain't he bad, bad Stacker Lee?"

"How big is dis bad, bad Stacker Lee?" John Henry asked her.

"Big enough to wound his finger around a forty-four gun," said the woman named Ruby. "Dat's all de big I wants to know how big he is."

"Whar do he live at?" John Henry asked her.

"Whar he's at," said Ruby. "On de river, over in Argenta, up on de hill, anywhar you sees dat Stacker Lee, well, dat's whar he is, 'cause he got a home anywhar he go."

"And he packs a forty-four gun, hunh?" said John Henry.

"And shoots a forty-four gun," said Ruby, "and de po-leece don't pay him no mind."

"Is de po-leece skeered of him?" John Henry asked her.

"De po-leece," said Ruby, "might not be skeered, but dey don't want no trouble."

"And he tuck a shot at poor you?" John Henry asked her.

"He shot my poor sister down," said Ruby, "and den tuck a shot at me."

"Well," said John Henry, "you go tell dat bad Stacker Lee dat big John Henry done come to town, so he kin lay his pistol down. Tell him John Henry is six foot tall and comes f'm he don't know whar. Tell him John Henry is big like a gi'nt and don't know his middle name. You go tell dat bad Stacker Lee about me, Ruby, 'cause me and him is liable to git crossed up."

And John Henry turned his back on Ruby and walked across the bridge to Argenta.

He went to a store and bought himself a new suit of clothes and a new pair of shoes. He bought a fancy shirt and a red necktie. Then he bought a four-dollar Stutson hat with a black hatband. " 'Cause I'm on my way to a funeral," he told the storekeeper, "and I wants to look big."

When he got all the fancy clothes on he went walking up the street, hunting for that bad Stacker Lee. And about the time he got up in front of Poor Selma's big two-story house at Third and Bird, he found him.

"You huntin' for me, podner?" said Stacker Lee.

"Maybe," said John Henry. "Is yo' name bad Stacker Lee?"

"Dat's de way de po-leece writes hit in de book," Stacker Lee told him, and he pulled out his forty-four gun and shot the shoestrings out of John Henry's shoes.

"De word I got," said John Henry, "say you totes a gun, so I reckon hit must be you."

"Must be," said Stacker Lee, and he shot the buttons off of John Henry's coat.

"De word I got," said John Henry, "say you shoots fast and straight."

"Kind of," said Stacker Lee, and he shot the hatband off of John Henry's Stetson hat.

"You's awful little and squinchy," said John Henry.

"Little," said Stacker Lee, "but loud." And he shot John Henry's necktie off.

"You gonter keep on wid dat shootin'," said John Henry, "to de fust thing you know you gonter git me ondressed. And when I gits ondressed I gits bad."

STACKER LEE

"I likes 'em bad," said Stacker Lee, and he shot John Henry's belt off.

So about that time Poor Selma heard all the racket out in front of her house and she came out to see what it was about. She saw Stacker Lee and John Henry standing still in the street, looking at each other, with John Henry's big arms bulging with strength and Stacker Lee's forty-four gun smoking. Then she counted the shoestrings and buttons and hatband and necktie and belt on the ground by John Henry.

"John Henry," she said, "dat bad Stacker Lee is done shot five shots at you and he ain't done you no harm. So whyn't you git on down de road before he gits mad and shoots dat last shot in yo' weary brain?"

"Would you bust down and cry," said John Henry, "efn he put dat last shot in my weary brain?"

"I likes you, John Henry," said Poor Selma. "You quit me like you was quittin' work, but I likes you mighty good. So don't let dat bad Stacker Lee lay yo' body down."

John Henry looked at Stacker Lee and then he looked at Poor Selma.

"Stacker Lee ain't gonter use dat last shot

at me," he said. "He might shoot you down and he might shoot hisse'f down, but he ain't gonter shoot big John Henry, 'cause he skeered he couldn't lay me down."

"I kin lay you down, big John Henry," said Stacker Lee.

"You might think you kin," said John Henry, "but you ain't so sho, and dat's how come you ain't gonter try. I might be bad and I might not be bad, but dat's what you don't know about me. You might shoot yo'se'f wid dat last shot, but you ain't gonter shoot big me, 'cause efn you shoots yo'se'f, you won't do nothin' but die. But efn you shoots me and don't lay me down, well, what you gonter do about dat, bad Stacker Lee? Shoot yo'se'f and you won't be nothin' but daid. But shoot me, and den what I'm gonter do to you? Maybe nothin' and maybe a heap, and dat's what you don't know about me. Efn you knowed you wouldn't be skeered, but you don't know nothin' about me."

So about that time Ruby walked up and saw Stacker Lee and big John Henry. "Dat's him, Stacker darlin'," said Ruby. "Mind out you don't let him git his hands on old sweet you."

"What you come buttin' in dis argyment

for?" Poor Selma asked Ruby. "I'll claw yo' eyes out efn you roots ag'in' John Henry."

"You John Henry's woman, hunh?" said Ruby. "Well, I'm bad Stacker Lee's woman, and I'm mighty nigh as bad as him," and she made a dive for Poor Selma.

So Poor Selma and Ruby had a big fight right in the street where John Henry and Stacker Lee were standing.

"Hit's one more shot in yo' gun," said John Henry.

"Hit is," said Stacker Lee, but he kept on watching the women fight.

"Maybe," said John Henry, "efn you laid me low you wouldn't need to put my shoestrings back in my shoes."

"I puts 'em back," said Stacker Lee. "I puts back de buttons and de tie and de hatband and de belt, too, 'cause I ain't got time to play wid you now. I'm watchin' dese ladies fight."

"Naw you ain't, bad Stacker Lee," said John Henry. "You's watchin' yo' liver turn upside down. Now gimme dat gun, you bad man, and gimme yo' watch and chain, 'cause you might be bad amongst de womenfo'ks, but you ain't so bad amongst me." And John Henry reached over and slapped bad old Stacker Lee just one time and he fell into the river.

"Crawl outn de river, you shovel-bill cat," said John Henry, "and I'll smack you in again!" And he slapped Stacker Lee back into the river. "You's powerful bad wid yo' tawk and yo' gun, but you ain't so bad wid me." And he slapped Stacker Lee so hard that it dried out his clothes.

"Now," said John Henry, "I'm gonter sing you a song dat you can't hear, and you don't know what hit means." So he sang him that bad John Henry song:

> "Stacker Lee was a bad man,
>   Twice as bad as he could be.
> Shot his woman wid a forty-four gun,
>   But he wouldn't take a shot at me, Lawd, Lawd.
>   And he wouldn't take a shot at me."

And then John Henry walked over and pulled the fighting women apart. "Y'all ladies quit dat rowin' and quarrelin'," he said, " 'cause yonder is Stacker Lee too skeered to fight about. And de onliest woman I lets fight about me don't live in dis town a-tall. So y'all ladies make up friends and remember kindly John Henry. I ain't no ladies' man and I won't be fit about. So stand back, you Argenta gals, and watch John Henry ramble, 'cause I'm big and bad and my home ain't hyar, 'cause hit's further down de road. I'm six foot tall and made outn meat, and I laid bad Stacker Lee down. So stand back, you gals and mens, and don't call me by my name, 'cause I'm f'm de Black River country whar de sun don't never shine, and my woman lives far away."

THE POOR SELMA "GRIS GRIS"

JOHN HENRY was a man and he was six feet
tall. But he ever had a woman on his weary
mind. Bad men crossed the field by another
path and the police couldn't see him at all. But
no matter where he rambled and where he
roamed, a woman would bear down on his soul.
So he went back to the Black River country
where he was born and he hunted up the old
witch woman.

"Old woman," he said, "you tawk to me and
you tawk straight."

"Tawkin' all de time, John Henry," said the
old witch woman. "You got a weary woman on
yo' mind and de doctor can't do you no good."

"I didn't come all de way back hyar," said
John Henry, "so's you c'd tell me somethin' I

already knowed. Tell me somethin' else, old woman."

The old woman put some brush on the fire and stuck her head in the smoke. "I smells Poor Selma," she said, "and she don't smell good to me."

"Now you's tawkin'," said John Henry. "But I quit Poor Selma like I'm quittin' work, and she hung her haid and cried."

"Yeah," said the old woman, "you quit her like you's quittin' work, John Henry, and dat's how de trouble start, 'cause, John Henry, you's a workin'man. You big and you bad and you been around, but you sho is a natchal workin'man."

"I kin quit work," said John Henry, "jest like I quit her."

"You kin," said the old witch woman, "but you can't stay quit. You can't quit work for long, and you can't quit Poor Selma for long, 'cause old ugly Selma pulled a stinger-ree on you and she mighty nigh laid you down."

"Stick yo' haid in de fire again," said John Henry, "and see what else you kin smell."

So the old woman stuck her head back in the fire and held it there for a long time.

"Can't see nothin' but Poor Selma," she said,

[93]

"and she looks mighty ugly. Her face is black and her mouf is big and her white teef is grinnin' at you. She say, 'Come back, John Henry, 'cause I ain't told you to go.' "

So John Henry got up and went outside and looked at the full moon. Then he came back into the house and sat down again. "Old woman," he said, "put some rose leaves in dat fire, and lay on some thyme and basil. Put fourteen blooms f'm de lilac bush, and a handful er black-eyed Susies."

So the old woman put all of that stuff on the fire and it blazed up and made solid red smoke.

"Git yo' haid in de chimney jam'," John Henry told her, "and see kin you smell somebody."

The old woman stuck her head back into the smoke and smelled. And then she took it out and looked at John Henry. "You got de blue gums and a cleavin' tongue and gray eyes like a conjure man," she told him, "or else, how come you work dem yarbs on de fire so's I kin see what I kin see?"

"Tell me what you kin see in dat solid red smoke," John Henry told the old woman.

"I sees a gal," the old woman said, "but she

ain't so tall and black. She lives down de river somewhars, and she's lookin' sweet in de eye at you."

"Dat'll be Julie Anne," John Henry said. "I left her layin' out thirty days in de jail. I ought to go pay her sweet fine."

"But Poor Selma is huntin' for you, too," said the old woman. "She's restless on yo' weary soul."

"I quit Poor Selma like I was quittin' work," John Henry said.

"But she ain't quit you," said the old woman. "She hit you wid dat stinger-ree, and de doctor can't he'p you out."

"S'posin'," said John Henry, "I went to N'Awlins and paid my darlin's fine?"

"You'd wawk away f'm her in four days," said the old woman, " 'cause you got Poor Selma on yo' mind."

"But I don't love Poor Selma good like I loves Julie Anne," said John Henry.

"Julie Anne might be yo' four-day fevers," said the old woman, "but Poor Selma is yo' wastin' disease. Julie Anne make you shiver and shake, but you forgits her too soon. But Poor Selma buried her stinger-ree in yo' soul and give you de weary all-overs."

"She claim she done many a man like dat," said John Henry, "but she claims I bowed her haid."

"You bowed her haid," said the old woman, "but she bowed yo' heart and soul."

So John Henry got up and went out to look at the stars.

"What do de stars say, John Henry?" the old woman asked him.

"Don't say nothin' but what you said," John Henry told her.

So the old woman put some mullen leaves on the fire and added some roots of sassafras.

"John Henry," said the old woman, "you's a man and you's made outn meat, and no kind er work kin harm you. But you tuck and let Poor Selma git you down and give you de 'way-down-yonders. Now make up yo' mind, John Henry, and don't make it up too hasty. Hit's one way I kin he'p you out, but hit's bound to cause you trouble. You got de sperits on yo' side, but de sperits come f'm de devil. So what do you say, John Henry? Do you want to be cyored er de Poor Selma habit? Well, you jest say de word.

"But listen at me tawkin' at you, John Henry. You's a big stout man, and you kin work all de time and git fat on de workin'. But bow yo' haid down jest one time and, John Henry, you's a goner. Bow yo' haid to man or god or let de job out-do you, and de fust news you gonter learn, old Cold Death gonter grab you. So what do you say, big John Henry? Kin you handle yo'se'f like a man and work or is you skeered to try hit? Hold yo' haid up too proud to bend, and you won't have no trouble. But bend yo' knees to god or man, and Cold Death gonter snatch you."

John Henry got up and walked around the house seven times. Then he went down to the river and drank seven swallows of water. Then he looked both ways twice as far as he could see, and then he came back to the house.

"I bows my haid to no man," said John Henry. "I'm six foot tall and I comes f'm de Black River country whar de sun don't never shine. So go on wid yo' ju-ju stuff, old woman. I'm a man and I holds my haid high. So come on wid yo' conjure."

The old woman got up and put some thorn sprouts on the fire, and then she poured seven buckets of river water on it. Then she shut her eyes and rocked back and forth in the chimney corner while she said:

> "Burn fire and squinch dis water.
> Crackle thawns, and crack Poor Selma.
> Rise free, smoke, and rise, John Henry."

Then she made John Henry pull off his shoes and stick his bare feet in the ashes. "Is you skeered, John Henry?" said the old woman. "De fire do git mighty hot sometime, and efn you ain't a man hit might burn you."

John Henry stuck his feet in the hot ashes. "Hit might burn," he said, "and hit might not. But I'm a man and fire won't hurt me. I wawks th'ough de fire and flame like I wawks th'ough de wind. Hit's all one and de same, 'cause I'm big and tall and my feet don't tetch de ground."

When John Henry said that the old woman turned around seven times and put a spell on John Henry. "Git goin', John Henry," she told him, " 'cause you's big and stout and yo' home ain't hyar, 'cause hits further down."

And about that time there was a mighty moaning and groaning that cleaved the air and made the whole world rock.

THE POOR SELMA "GRIS GRIS"

"Dat'll be Poor Selma," said the old woman, " 'cause I put de dead spell on her. And when Poor Selma laid down and died, de last words I heard her groan was, 'John Henry, don't you grieve after me.' "

"How come I grieve after her," said John Henry, " 'cause she ain't no gal er mine."

"Well," said the old woman, "dat's de way I likes to hyar you tawk. Now I bet you goin' to yo' Julie Anne and hang yo' hat in de hall."

"I'll th'ow my shoes under de bed and make myse'f at home."

"Mind out, John Henry," said the old witch woman. "Julie Anne love you good, but she gonter kill you sho. She can't he'p lovin' you and she can't he'p killin' you. You love wid her and she love wid you, but y'all ain't gonter be happy. You gonter hurt her and she gonter kill you, and den you bofe'll be sorry. But hit ain't none er mine, John Henry," said the old witch woman. "Hit's yo' own hawg-killin', so hold up yo' haid and travel."

But John Henry didn't hear what she said. He was already on the way to his woman. He walked out in the middle of the road and he sang his song at the full moon:

JOHN HENRY

"I looked up high and I looked down low,
  Jest to see what I could see.
Couldn't see nothin' but my Julie Anne,
  And she couldn't see nothin' but me, Lawd, Lawd,
  And she couldn't see nothin' but me."

MAN'S EVER BURDEN

J OHN HENRY found the Black River country
warm and lazy, with Poor Selma off his
weary mind and no work to do. He lay
around in the shade awhile and then he lay in
the sunshine. The woodpeckers in the dead gum
trees beat out dull music for his ears, and the
bullfrogs in the brakes sang bass. The crickets
in the weeds fiddled night and day, and the
roosters crowed in the mornings.

"I been workin' and I been playin'," said John
Henry, "so now I'm gonter rest my weary soul.
I been hongry and I been cold, so now I'm gonter
'suage my stomach. So bring me some victuals,
old woman, and bring 'em plenty hot. Bring
me some turnip greens piled so high I can't see

de top, and ridge 'em down wid middlin'. Range
my cabbages around me like a fence, wid hog
shanks for de fence posts. Make me a pone er
cownbread so big I can't see de top, and mix in
a ba'l er cracklin's, 'cause I'm a hongry man
and I aims to eat some victuals."

The old woman looked at John Henry and
then she looked out the window. "Dem sounds
like man victuals," she said. "Victuals for a
natchal man."

"My name is John Henry," he told her, "and
I'm six foot tall. I must be a man."

So the old woman didn't say a word. She got
up and went into her garden. She cut down one
stalk of sugar cane and peeled one joint for
John Henry. "Dat's for you, son," she said.
"Dat's for a big man like you. And efn hit's too
rough for yo' mouf inside, well, I'll git some
sugar in a rag and make you a sugar tit, 'cause
sugar tits is for a man yo' size, John Henry.
You's big and tall, but you's a baby in yo'
mind. You gripes when de gals git sweet after
you and you lays around in de sunshine. When
a baby ain't but six months old, dat's de way he
acks, so I reckon you's a baby."

When the old woman made that talk to John

Henry he got mad! "Don't make me mad, old witchin' woman," John Henry told her, "or else I might bust up somethin'. Don't let me git my Af'ican up, or I'm liable to wreck and ruin you, 'cause I'm big and I'm bad and I been around. I worked and I played and now I'm fixin' to rest some. So don't make me out no baby, old woman, 'cause John Henry is my name and I'm six foot tall."

The old woman just looked at John Henry and laughed away down in her stomach.

"John Henry," she said, "hit ain't for a man to rest. A baby, yes. But when a baby grows up de burden grows up wid him. Weary and trouble and sorrow and work you gits aplenty. But hit ain't no rest in de sack for a man and you can't lay yo' burden down. You's bawn wid a burden growin' on yo' back, and you totes hit to yo' dyin' day. You kin work and play, but you can't rest, 'cause de burden grows on yo' poor shoulders. De path is befo' you, but hit's full er sand and gravel. De wawkin' ain't easy, once you's a man."

John Henry looked a long time at the old woman, and then he went out and looked at the river. It was clear and cool and filled with quiet.

But it wouldn't tell him the answer. So he came back and asked the old woman. "Old woman," he said, "how come is a man bawn when hit ain't nothin' but work and weary? How come a man can't be a man widout all de burden?"

"Efn I told you dat," the old woman said, "den you'd know mo'n me. Hit jest de way things come and de way things go, and hit ain't none er my doin's. Some say one thing and some say another, but hit all 'mounts up to one and de same. Hyar you is, and hyar's yo' burden, so I can't witch hit f'm you. So git yo' hat, John Henry, and git about de country. Git you a shovel or a mule or a cotton hook or a woman. Hit's all one and de same. You got to weary yo' life along, 'cause dat's de way hit turns out. You work and yo' back gits tired; you lay round hyar in de sun and shade and yo' soul gits twice as weary. Take a job er work, and you wear cawns in yo' hands. Th'ow yo' shoes under some woman's bed, and cawns come on yo' weary soul. Quit yo' work, and you gits de all-overs. Quit yo' woman, and you gits de down-yonders. Hit's all one and de same, John Henry. So git yo' hat and keep a-movin', son, 'cause hit ain't no rest for de weary."

MAN'S EVER BURDEN

So John Henry got his hat, but he sat back down on the doorstep. "Tell me, old woman," he said, "ain't hit some way to git around and not bear my burden? Can't a man be a man when he's big like me? How come hit ain't no rest for de weary?"

The old woman looked at John Henry and then she laughed. "Son," she said, "ev'y step you takes is jest one mo' step. You can't onstep hit. You kin back-step and you kin side-step, but hit's two things gonter be wid you. No matter whar you go or whar you turn you gonter have company. Yo' burden and yo' shadow gonter be right along, John Henry. So git yo' hat and git around. You th'owed yo' shoes under Poor Selma's bed, and den you wawked out on her. But she stayed wid you to I *gris-grised* her off, but you still got a burden."

"I quit Poor Selma like I quits work," said John Henry.

"Yeah," said the old woman, "you quit her like you quit a job er work. But you bound to go back to some yuther job er work, or you's bound to go back to some yuther woman. You quit Poor Selma, son, but she's all you quit. You quit a job er steamboatin', and dat's all you quit. You quit a job er steamboatin' and got a job er firin'. You quit a gal named Poor Selma, and you got a gal named Julie Anne."

"I'm long gone f'm Julie Anne," said John Henry.

"In yo' mind, yeah," said the old woman. "But in yo' heart, no. You got on yo' hat, right now, and yo' heel is eetchin' for N'Awlins. You's on yo' way, son, 'cause you seed her and you tuck yo' choice, John Henry. To you chose her out, you was a free man to work or play or lay around. But you tuck yo' choice, and dar she is."

"Listen, old woman," John Henry said. "You do a mighty heap er tawkin', but you's tawkin' to a man. I'm big and I'm black and I treads strange ground when I travels. So how come I'm gittin dis tawk-tawk f'm you? How come I ain't a man er my own? You's a fool, old woman."

"Tawk wid yo' tongue," said the old woman, "but you jest sayin' words. You might git around dis land er heap, but you still gonter be John Henry. Hit might be one job or hit might be two. And hit might be one woman, or hit might be a hund'ed. But yo' burden and yo' shadow gonter stick to you as long as you stands up like a man."

"Efn I kin take my choice about work and women," said John Henry, "how come I can't take my choice and not take na'n?"

"Did you take yo' choice about bein' bawn?" said the old woman. "And about bein' bawn in de Black River country whar de sun don't never shine?"

"Den efn I didn't," said John Henry, "well, how come I was bawn?"

The old woman looked at John Henry, and then she got up and put some wood on the fire. "Ah, Lawd, John Henry," she said, "Ah, Lawd."

"Tawk to me, old woman," John Henry said, " 'cause I'm gittin' mad and I'm liable to wrop you around somethin' and break yo' neck. I wants straight tawk. I'm sick and tired er yo' ju-ju."

"Ah, Lawd," said the old woman. "You might break my bones and lay me cold in death, but dat don't answer no question. So put on yo' hat, son, and lace up yo' shoes and start to gittin'

around. An remember what I said about standin'
up like a man, 'cause do you bow yo' haid you
won't be no man no more. Hold up yo' haid
and be a man, and bow yo' haid and die. Be a
man, John Henry, and work and play. But you
can't lay around. Sing you a song whilst you
work, and sing one whilst you play, 'cause you's
big and bad and yo' skin is black and you got
to tote yo' burden. Hit might be work on yo'
poor shoulders, or hit might be a woman on
yo' poor soul. But hit's gonter follow you down
de line. Hit might be quick and hit might be long
befo' you lays hit down. But hit'll be wid you
to you lays out cold, 'cause hit ain't no rest for
de weary."

John Henry stood up and looked toward the
east. Then he looked at the old woman sitting
in the jamb of the chimney. "Old woman," he
said, "you tawks crooked like a snake, but I
reckon you knows John Henry. I ain't skeered
er work and I ain't skeered er women. I kin
handle myse'f on any job, and I kin handle de
women. I got a gal down in N'Awlins, and I
knows about a job in Natchez. Now you watch
me. Is bad old John Henry gonter go to his

woman or is he gonter go to dat job er work?
Now what you gonter say?" And he strutted
up and down in front of the house like he was
fixing to say his say-so. "I'm gonter git my
woman and take her wid me and git dat job,"
he said. "Dat's de way wid John Henry. A job
might weary a poor man down, and a woman
might run him crazy, but I kin handle a job
and a gal and not know nothin' tetched me!
So stand back, all you bullies, and watch big
old John Henry! Stand back and let me git my
gal, and den let me git to workin', 'cause I'm
big and bad and black and mean and my feet
don't tetch de ground!" And John Henry
walked away from the old witch woman in the
Black River country and struck out for Julie
Anne down in New Orleans.

But before he got down the path the old
woman put a thorn bush in the fire and she stuck
her head in the smoke. "John Henry is a man,"
she said, "but he do ack brash. Efn de thawns
kin stick in his back and de smoke git in his
eye, well, he kin handle de job and de woman."
So she stuck a thorn in her arm and the smoke
got in her eye. It hurt but she didn't say a word.
She sang:

JOHN HENRY

"John Henry was about six foot tall
  And I reckon he was a man.
He didn't fear no job er work,
  But he loved his Julie Anne, Lawd, Lawd,
  And dey bofe went hand-in-hand."

HAND IN HAND

THE first time John Henry went away from
the Black River country he thought he
was a man. But he wasn't. He was big and stout
and had an itching heel for travel. But he hadn't
done any getting around. Life was where he was,
and work was what he was doing. That was all
he knew about it. But the women and the work
began to bear down on him and the old woman
told him he'd have to bear his burden.

The second time John Henry went away from
the Black River country he had a burden on his
shoulder and a woman on his mind. The burden
was endless jobs of work and the woman on his
mind was a girl named Julie Anne that he walked
away from, down in New Orleans.

There was something else bearing down on

JOHN HENRY

John Henry when he left the Black River country, too. It was a mark put in his soul by the
old woman when she used the *gris gris* to free
him from Poor Selma. "Ev'y time you *gris gris*
somethin' off," the old woman told him, "well,
you turn right around and *gris gris* somethin'
else on. So hold up yo' haid, son," she told him,
"and be a man. Or else, bend yo' neck and die."

So John Henry got along out of the Black
River country and he went to New Orleans to
see his Julie Anne. He walked up to the door and
knocked. But the door was locked! "Dat ain't
right," he said. "Dis door ain't jue to be locked
ag'in' me."

But over across the street there was a girl
named Ruby, and when she saw John Henry
knocking on Julie Anne's door she sang him a
song:

"Well, hit's been some changes made since you been gone.
  Lawd, hit's been some changes made since you been gone.
    Got home dis mawnin' at four o'clock,
    Knocked on de door and de door was locked.
    H'ist up de window, poke in-a yo' haid.
    They's a great big stranger in de foldin'-bed,
  'Cause they's been some changes made since you been
    gone!"

"What kind er song dat you singin' at me?" John Henry asked her.

"Hello, John Henry!" said Ruby. "Is dat you?"

"Must be," said John Henry. "I'm standin' hyar tawkin'."

"And I bet you huntin' for dat low-down Julie Anne, ain't you?" Ruby asked him.

"Must be," said John Henry. "I'm knockin' on her door."

"She's long gone," said Ruby. "Whyn't you come on over to my house, John Henry, and lemme tell you all about dat gal?"

So John Henry went over to Ruby's house and sat down.

"Hang up yo' hat in de hall, darlin'," said Ruby, "and th'ow yo' shoes under de bed. Make yo'se'f easy around de house, 'cause dis is whar big old you gonter live at."

"My hat's restin' easy on my haid," said John Henry, "and my shoes don't pinch my feets. So come on, old ugly gal, and tell me whar Julie Anne gone at."

"I reckon she must be yo' Julie Anne," said Ruby. "She's ev'ybody else's Julie Anne and I don't see how come she ain't you'n, too. But I reckon she off right now wid a nigger named Sam."

John Henry looked at Ruby and then he loked out the window. Ruby was black and bony and ugly, and the street outside was knee-high with weeds. "You tryin' to put my woman in de dozens?" John Henry asked her.

"Not me," said Ruby. "She was in de dozens long befo' I ever hyared her name. Dat gal is too low down ——"

"She'll come back quick as she hyars I'm in town," John Henry said.

"Maybe," said Ruby. "But can't nobody never tell about dat gal. Sometime she do and sometime she don't. But me, I never would come back, 'cause I wouldn't run off. So come on, Big Stuff, and hang yo' hat in de hall and th'ow yo' shoes under my foldin'-bed, cause Julie Anne is long gone and I'm yo' woman now."

Ruby talked fast and she said a heap and John Henry didn't say a word. He just listened at Ruby's talk. But the first thing he knew his head got hot and his shoes started pinching his feet. "Look like you puttin' de word on me, baby," he told her, "but you ain't de gal for me."

"I'm wid you, ain't I?" Ruby asked him. "Den

HAND IN HAND

I'm yo' woman, 'cause de woman which is present is de onliest woman to know. So come on and pick yo' woman, John Henry, and pick one close around. Sometime a big purty ricebird fly in f'm de swamps and sets on de wires by de house. She mighty purty to look at, preenin' and twistin' and carryin' on. But de fust thing you know, she done flew away. Den she ain't purty no more."

"I'd fly off wid her," said John Henry, and he stood up and sang a song:

"Good-by, good-by, my Ruby gal,
    And I hopes you's feelin' fine,
'Cause I'm f'm de Black River country
    Whar de sun don't never shine, Lawd, Lawd,
    Whar de sun don't never shine."

And he got up and walked out of the house. "So long, Ruby," he said. "I'll see you soon."

When he got out in the street he looked up and he saw Julie Anne walking straight toward him.

"Hy-dy, darlin'!" said John Henry. "I been huntin' for you."

"I don't live in Ruby's house," said Julie Anne.

"Ruby say you went off wid a nigger name Sam," John Henry told her.

"Ruby say a heap," said Julie Anne.

"Did you?" said John Henry.

"Do you see me wid a nigger named Sam?" Julie Anne asked him.

"I didn't see you in yo' own house," said John Henry.

Julie Anne didn't say a word. She just walked along and sang:

"I wisht I was a little bird.
    I'd fly over de mountain-top so high.
  Den I'd weep like a willow and moan like a dove,
    Den I'd lay my burden down and die, Lawd, Lawd,
    And lay my weary burden down and die."

"Yeah," said John Henry, "but you got to hold up yo' haid."

"Efn I was a man," said Julie Anne, "I'd hold up my haid. But I ain't no man, so I kin hang my haid and cry."

They walked on down the street for a long ways. John Henry knew what he was thinking about in his mind, but he couldn't find the words to tell her, and Julie Anne knew what she was thinking, but she was tongue-tied, too.

HAND IN HAND

So finally when they got to the house, John Henry took the key and unlocked the door. He walked inside and hung his hat in the hall. Then he took his shoes off and pitched them under the bed. Then he took Julie Anne by the right hand and sang to her:

> "I'm big and black and six foot tall
> And my feet don't tetch de ground.
> So I takes my gal by her right hand,
> 'Cause I aims to git around, Lawd, Lawd,
> Yes, I'm fixin' to git around."

"Sho is," said Julie Anne, "but you jest set down in de cheer and wait to I gits back, darlin'." And she got up and left the house.

Pretty soon there was a knock on the door, but John Henry didn't say a word. So there was another knock and a man said: "Open up de door, darlin'. Dis is Sam."

John Henry didn't say a word.

"Go on and open up de door," said Sam. "Dat nigger named John Henry ain't studdin' you. He done come back and tuck up wid a gal name' Ruby. You know old slew-foot Ruby, live acrost de street? Well, dat's who yo' big man is tuck up wid. So come on, baby, and open up de door. Be sweet to me and forgit dat old country boy."

So when John Henry heard that talk he got mad. But he bit his tongue and squeezed his throat until his voice sounded like a woman's. So he said, "Hold on a minute, darlin', to I finds de key."

So John Henry got up and unlocked the door. And Sam walked in like a coon in a steel trap!

"Don't make me mad, Sam," John Henry told him, " 'cause I'm big and bad and I'm hard to handle." And he grabbed that nigger named Sam by the throat and choked him until his tongue flopped liked a bell-clapper. "Don't never lie on me to my woman, Sam," he said, " 'cause I can't stand bein' lied on." And he doubled up his fist and hit Sam on the jaw. "Don't try to creep on me when I'm ramblin' around," he said, " 'cause I'm fixin' to live hyar wid my woman and I won't want to tear de house down." So he grabbed Sam by the heels and he knocked down the rafters with Sam's head. "And don't hang around me, Sam," he said, " 'cause you don't b'long in dis shanty." And he threw Sam out the window.

After a long time Julie Anne came back.

"Don't tear de house down, darlin'," she told him, " 'cause us is fixin' to live hyar."

John Henry reached out and took Julie Anne by the hand again. But he dropped it right quick.

"What's all dat hay and grapes doin' in yo' hand, baby?" he said.

"I don't know," said Julie Anne. "I been over tawkin' to Ruby about you, some, and dat might not be hay and grapes. Dat might be hair and eyeballs."

"Well," said John Henry, "you can't pick Sam up wid a shovel, and dis house ain't fitten for kindlin'-wood, so us might as well be gittin' around some. I'm fixin' to find me a job er work. So come on, you good-lookin' woman, and follow John Henry around." And then he sang to her:

> "Grab yo' bundle and grab yo' hat,
>   And grab yo' dress er red.
> Grab yo' man by his-a right hand,
>   And follow whar's you's led, Lawd, Lawd,
>   'Cause you hyared what I said."

She took him by the right hand and sang back at him:

JOHN HENRY

"Grab my hat and grab my bundle
And grab my dress er blue.
Grab my man by his right hand.
I'm gonter follow you, Lawd, Lawd,
I'm gonter follow you."

SHOULDER YOUR LOAD AND WALK

WHEN John Henry left Saratoga Street with his Julie Anne by his side he was a happy man. "Us is goin' whar hit's a job er work, baby," he said. "I hyared old man Billie Bob Russell was layin' down de steel on de Yaller Dog railroad up by Natchez, and old Billie Bob pays a dollar a day."

"Anywhar you says, John Henry," Julie Anne told him. "You go and den turn around and you see me standin' at yo' side. All de time like dat, John Henry. F'm now on, hunh? 'Cause I loves you so good."

They went down to the river landing and John Henry went up to the mate of the *Big Jim White*. "Hy-dy, Cap'm," he said. "I'm John Henry and I wants a job, I comes f'm de Black

River country whar all de good rousterbouts comes f'm, and I'm gittin' up to Natchez for a job er work. I needs to roust my way up de river."

"Roust, John Henry," the big mate told him. "You roust at the landings and I'll pay you six bits and board."

So John Henry got in line, ready to roust freight on the *Big Jim White*. But when he got in line he saw that nobody but men were rousting, and he knew Julie Anne couldn't roust. So he went back to the mate.

"I got a woman, too, Cap'm," he said.

"A woman can't roust," said the mate.

"She kin maid on de boat," said John Henry.

"Too many maids now," said the mate. "Every nigger on the main deck wants to haul his woman round as a maid. Can't haul your woman, John Henry. I can haul you, but if your woman rides she's got to pay her fare."

"Us ain't got no money to pay de fare," said John Henry.

"Then," said the mate, "leave her at home."

"Ain't got no home," John Henry said. "Dat's how come us goin' up to Natchez, 'cause my home got tored down."

SHOULDER YOUR LOAD AND WALK

"Leave your woman here, then," said the mate, "and find you a new one up at Natchez. A big buck like you ought to find a woman anywhere he goes."

John Henry went back and got in line. He saw Julie Anne sitting on a sack of sweet sugar by the gangplank. She was waiting for him to tell her to go on board. He looked at her and then he looked at the other women standing around, waiting for their men to tell them to get on board. So he sang himself a little song:

"I ain't never gonter stay married.
And I ain't gonter settle down.
'Cause I can find me a sweet woman
In mighty nigh any town, Lawd, Lawd,
So I'll ramble round and round."

Then John Henry went to work rousting freight down the stage. And while he rousted freight Julie Anne sat on the sweet-sugar sack and waited. Every time he went up the plank he passed her and every time he went down he passed her. But he just passed her by. " 'Cause a woman," he said, "is too much trouble for a good man to haul around, and I got to git around de country."

But about that time there was a big nigger named Sam rousting in the line and Sam went up to Julie Anne.

"Hello, baby," Sam told her. "Big lump er black sugar, settin' on a big sack er white sugar."

"No mind what is settin' on which," Julie Anne told him. "And no mind is I'm sugar or is I'm black. You jest tote yo' load, son, and leave me be."

Sam laughed and put his finger on Julie Anne's cheek and then put it in his mouth. "Sho is sweet, baby," he said. Then he put his finger in the sugar sack, and put it in his mouth. "You so sweet, darlin'," he said, "you makes dis sugar taste bitter as gall."

John Henry saw that, but he was aiming to leave poor Julie Anne behind, so he didn't say anything. But it worried him to hear Sam going on like that.

"I wish dat gal didn't bear down on me no harden den dis freight I'm totin'," he said. "But dat good-lookin' heifer bear down so hard on my weary mind." But he didn't do anything about it; he just kept right on toting his freight.

But the next time around he heard Sam talking low to Julie Anne. "When de boat pull out,"

SHOULDER YOUR LOAD AND WALK

Sam told her, "well, I'm stayin' behind, jest like you is. And me and you gonter take dese wages I'm makin' and us is gonter spend 'em all over town. Me and you, hunh, baby?"

Julie Anne looked at Sam and then she looked at big John Henry. She didn't say a word. She just hung her head and sang a song:

> "Ef I travel wid my lovin' man,
>   How kin I travel wid you?
> But efn John Henry leave me settin' hyar,
>   What kin a poor gal do, Lawd, Lawd,
>   And I might good-time wid you."

When John Henry heard that song he got mad. "Don't make me mad, woman," he said. "Who gonter leave you behind? What you singin' songs at dat Sam for? Ain't you fixin' to git around wid me? I said I was gittin' around wid you, and dat's what I means."

"I said I was gittin around wid you, too, darlin'," said Julie Anne. "But you's big and bad and kin find a woman anywhar you go. And how kin I roust my way up the river wid you? And efn I can't roust, who gonter pay my steamboat fare?"

"Don't ax me how, gal," John Henry told

her. "Don't ax me why. But I'm John Henry and I'm six foot tall and my feets don't touch de ground. And efn I say's I'm takin' you wid me, sweet thing, well, just watch old John Henry."

Then John Henry went up to the mate and told him; he said, "Cap'm, is I'm a good rouster?"

"You are, John Henry," said the mate. "You're from the Black River country, and you're the best rouster in the line. But a rouster can't make but six bits a day and board."

"S'posin'," said John Henry, "I take dem six bitses and pays my woman's steamboat fare up to Natchez?"

"A rouster's wages," said the mate, "won't pay a woman's fare but halfway to Natchez. She'll have to walk halfway. You'd have to be two men to haul your woman around."

"I'm two times as good a rouster as dat nigger named Sam, ain't I?" said John Henry.

"You may be," said the mate, "but Sam stays in line, and he totes a sack of sugar on every time you do."

So John Henry made one more go-round. The big sack of sugar he toted weighed two hundred pounds. But it didn't bear down on him like poor little Julie Anne did.

"Do I tote two sacks er sugar," said John Henry, "whilst dat nigger named Sam is totin' only jest one, den do I gits two-times on my wages?"

"If you're man enough to do it," said the mate.

So John Henry looked at Julie Anne and then he looked at the driver. "Load me down, you sugar-lifters," he said, " 'cause I'm two men rolled up in one and I'm drawin' down two men's wages. I got a sack er sugar on my back and a sack er sugar on my weary mind. So put two sacks on my back and stand out er my way, you bullies. Stand back, you Sam, and leave me pass. Double work and double wages, 'cause my sweet Julie Anne got to ride de boat. Load me down, you h'isters. Put a two hund'ed pound sack on my right shoulder, and put a two hund'ed pound sack on my left shoulder, 'cause I'm big John Henry and I'm tree-top tall, and I hauls my woman around."

"Tawks like a Black River rouster," said the driver, "and he built like a man and he kin haul his woman round. But you, John Henry, listen to a old river nigger f'm de Black River land whar de sun don't never shine."

"Say on, driver, say on," said John Henry, " 'cause I kin stand hyar loaded down like a four-mule wagon and listen at yo' tawk."

"Well," said the driver, "befo' yo' time and befo' my time hit was a big rousterbout named Sam. Sam was big and bad and six foot tall, and he hauled his woman round. But Sam is long daid, now, and his woman got a brand new man, 'cause Sam worked double to pay her fare, but he didn't made no wages. And how you gonter buy a woman a dress and what she gonter eat durin' de lay-off? You's big and stout like two men, and what you gonter do for wages? You works double and pays her fare, but a gal got to buy some dresses. Two men kin haul a woman around, but hit's always some yuther man makin' de wages which gonter git dat woman. You spent yo' time payin' her steamboat fare, and what you gonter do for a cook stove? Some nigger wid a dollar in his hand come right along behind you, and de first thing you know yo' gal is gone and you can't do nothin' about hit."

John Henry stood and listened to the river man's talk until finally he got the idea. It took two men to haul a woman and a third man to keep her happy!

"Dat's me," said John Henry. "I might look like one big man, and I might look like two men. But pitch another sack er sugar somewhar on me, and watch me make dese wages. I'm haulin' my gal up de river and I aims to haul her right. Efn hit takes one man to haul a woman, well, dat'll be a man named me. Efn hit takes two men to haul a gal, well, dey call dat man John Henry. And efn hit takes three men to make her happy, well, dem men will be my mama's son. So pile dat sugar high on my haid whilst I makes three men's wages. Pile hit up tree-top high, and stiddy me down de gangplank. Tell de cook to feed me three times, 'cause I'm three men all in one. And tell de Cap'm to pay me my wages like my name was three names long.

"So git on de boat, you Julie Anne, and git out er my way you bullies. I'm a roustin' fool f'm I don't know whar, and my feets don't tetch de ground. Pile up de sugar on my weary back, and ease my heartfelt burden. Sing me a song whilst I coonjines down, and grab me when I gits dar, 'cause I'm a ramblin' rouster and I can't be stopped." And he coonjined down the plank, singing:

> "Pile my tote-load tree-top high,
>   'Cause I'm roustin' all de time.
>   D'ruther have a burden on my poor back,
>   Den a woman on my weary mind, Lawd, Lawd,
>   Den a woman on my weary mind."

And that big John Henry from the Black River country danced down the gangplank carrying six hundred pounds of sugar on his head and shoulders, making three men's wages, all for his Julie Anne!

JOHN HENRY'S PATHWAY

WHEN the *Big Jim White* pulled out from New Orleans that hot summer day she was loaded smokestack high with sugar. And on top of the highest sack stood big John Henry, bowing to the people on the bank and tipping his hat to the ladies.

" 'Cause I'm a man and I'm gittin' around," he said. "I'm big and work don't hurt me. I'm two men and I'm haulin' my woman wid me, 'cause I'm big and stout and I rousts like I don't know what. Sugar in a sack and sugar in a dress, hit's all one and de same. So stand back, you river rats, and lay low, you dirt-eaters, 'cause I'm haulin' my Julie Anne wherever I goes and my feet don't tetch de ground."

[131]

But while John Henry was making his say-so on top of the sugar, the big old driver of the *Big Jim White* was listening and looking. "You better lay down, son," he said. "You brash now and you's loaded sugar. But hit's a woman gonter take ev'ything you got and beg for more. So lay down, you rouster, and rest yo' weary bones."

"How come I better lay down?" John Henry asked him. "I ain't sick and I ain't tired and I ain't built for restin'. All dat sugar I been roustin' jest make my muscles soople. Efn dis boat two times as big as hit is, I wouldn't mo'n git up a sweat, 'cause my bones is made outn solid steel and my muscles is made outn rubber. Hit takes three sacks er sugar to git a spring in my knees and make a song in my shoulder."

Then John Henry pranced and talked all over the top of that big pile of sugar, making his say-so to the people.

"He might be Samson and he might be Goliar," the people said, "but he tawks like big John Henry."

Now John Henry was big and he was a man, but the *Big Jim White* was a steamboat on the river. John Henry was riding the *Big Jim White* but the *White* was riding the river. And all the while John Henry was standing so high on that sugar, making his man-talk to the people the *Big Jim White* was riding on the river, dipping her big sidewheels in the bosom of the old witch and stirring up plat-eyes. So the first thing anybody knew, the river whispered a song to the steamboat and the steamboat rocked like a cradle, and the steamboat rocked John Henry. Until the first thing John Henry knew he heard a big brass band playing a sweet song behind the stars, and he thought it was his poor old mamma singing:

> "When John Henry was a little bitty boy
> And a-settin' on his mamma's knee,
> Said he'd git around like a natchal man,
> But he'd have to shet his eyes to see, Lawd, Lawd,
> And he'd have to sleep and dream to see."

So John Henry sat down and closed his eyes while the old river rocked a sweet dream into John Henry's big stout body.

The dream came up and sat down by John Henry and took him by the right hand. "John Henry," said the dream, "don't mind me, 'cause I ain't nothin' but a dream. But shet yo' eyes,

son, and look at what I'm fixin' to show you.
You ain't one man, son, but you's three. You's
one man to pay yo' fare, and you's one man to
pay yo' woman's fare, and you's one man to
make yo' wages. Dat makes three men, 'cause
a man got to make wages or else he ain't no
man."

"I knows all about dat," said John Henry.
"I'm makin' my wages."

"You's bound for up-de-river, John Henry,"
the dream told him, "and you's takin' yo' woman
along. Well, dat's de way for a man to do. Anybody kin git around by hisse'f, but hit takes a
man to handle a woman and a job at de same
time."

"Say on," said John Henry.

"Look twarge de nawth, John Henry," said
the dream. "Look and see all dat big wages!
Look at you in dat big Stutson hat, a-ridin' in
dat coach-and-four, wid all de people bowin' and
givin' you hy-dy when you go by! Do dat suit
yo' taste, son?"

"I'm ridin' by myse'f in dat coach-and-four,"
said John Henry. "Ain't hit no woman kin ride
wid me? 'Cause hit ain't no fun to ride by
myse'f."

JOHN HENRY'S PATHWAY

So the dream turned John Henry around and pointed to the south. "Looky yonder, John Henry," said the dream. "See all er dem women swarmin' around you? All dressed up in store-bought dresses wid high-heel shoes and stockin's, and makin' a fuss over big old you and carryin' on so scandalous? Look at Ruby in dat big white hat wid a bird fixin' to fly offn hit! And yonder Delia and Poor Selma, too, standin' around and gigglin'! And a heap more gals you ain't never seen, makin jokes and laughin'!"

But John Henry shook his head. "Dat don't suit my taste," he said, "and I don't like all de chatter-chatter. Women chatter like a old guinea hen and dey don't say nothin' I likes to listen at."

So the dream pointed toward the east. "Look at all dem gamblin'-men wid dey big box coats and dey neckties. Th'owin' dem dice and shufflin' dem cyards, and bein' big stuff round de corn-ders! How you like all er dat stuff, John Henry?"

"I gambles," said John Henry, "and I wins and I loses. But I don't like dem gamblers. Hit's all too much er de same old thing and de same old thing gits tiresome."

"Den," said the dream, "look twarge de west

[135]

and see what you see and tell me does you like hit. Look at big old you in dat big box coat wid de horseshoe pin and de necktie. Wid you Stutson hat on de back er yo' haid, a-struttin' amongst de ladies. One gal or a dozen on yo' tracks and you can't hardly fight 'em offn you. 'Cause you's big and handsome and you's got a way, and de ladies can't give you de go-by."

"Dem clothes looks good, and de gals looks nice, but look at dem big yaller shoes! Yaller shoes pinches my feets and a standin' collar chokes me."

So the dream led John Henry away to the edge of the boat and pointed straight to heaven. "Look at dem wings and dat golden harp and dat big diamond bass hawn. Look at dem silver pots and pans, and look at all de sweet victuals. Hyar de singin' er songs er Zion, and hyar de gospel preachin'."

But John Henry shook his head. "Nawp," he said, "de saints is kneelin' and I'm a man and I don't kneel to nothin'. And I got to have my victuals plain all cooked down in a iron kittle, wid a heap er side meat to season hit down, and cawnbread to get de potlicker."

Then the dream pointed straight down to hell,

and asked John Henry what about it. "Look at dat cocaine and happy dust, and look at de drinkin' licker! Look at de gamblers all makin' dey jokes, and look at de spo'tin' ladies! And look at de smoke comin' f'm de pit, and look at de fire in de middle. Look at old Satan all r'ared back, a-stirrin' de sinners wid a pitchfawk! And look at old you, punchin' dem chunks to keep de fire er burnin'! Well, John Henry, hit looks like you got work and play in hell, efn you jest go after hit. And hit's a broomstone fire to cook yo' victuals and hell is full er middlins."

"Look kind er good, and hit look kind er bad," John Henry told the dream. "Maybe I'd like hit and maybe I won't, but let me look up de river. Now, looky yonder at my Julie Anne a-b'ilin' down my victuals. Look at dat sweet gal in dat tent whilst I'm workin' on de railroad. Look at old me wid a hammer in my hand and makin' dem spikes go down! Hyar dat hammer ring out a song and see hit shine like silver!

"Ain't no hammer kin ring like mine,
    You kin hyar hit all around.
Shine like silver and she ring like gold,
    And she weighs nine solid pound, Lawd, Lawd,
    And she weighs nine solid pounds.

"Dat," said John Henry, "is what I'm doin' so I opens up my eyes and I won't see no more."

Then John Henry woke up. It was night and the moon was yellow like gold. He turned around to find Julie Anne, but she wasn't by his side. Then he got up and walked about, and he found her sitting down in a dark place, talking to a big nigger named Sam.

"I thought you wa'n't never gonter wake up," she told him. "And I been tawkin' to a friend er mine named Sam."

"How long you been tawkin' to Sam?" John Henry asked her.

"Not for long," Julie Anne said. "Sam he went to sleep quick as he got on de boat and den he got his sleep out and so he woke up and started tawkin' to me. But you, you was braggin' about how big and stout you was, and den you didn't git yo' sleep out for so long I got lonesome."

That made John Henry mad. "Look out, woman," he said; "don't make me mad. I been workin' like three men to haul you on dis boat, and dat de way you do me. I works for me and I works for you and I works to make de wages. But dat ain't enough for you, hunh, gal? You skeered you gonter git lonesome! What kind er thing is you, gal? What do hit take to please you? You come on hyar or I'll wring yo' neck and chunk you in de river!" And John Henry grabbed his woman and dragged her away from Sam.

Then he sat down beside her and watched the moon get high in the night and turn everything to silver. The *Big Jim White* dipped up a sweet song and sent it up to them.

But the wise old driver shook his head, for he knew all about John Henry. And he knew all about Julie Anne, too, because Julie Anne was a woman. "He's a man," said the driver, "and dat ain't no lie. But Julie Anne's a woman. So set close and watch de moon rise high, 'cause hit gits hot at daylight. You's restin' now, but you's loaded down, and yo' burden sho is heavy. Hit ain't on yo' back, but hit's on yo' soul, so John Henry, God bless you."

RING, STEEL, RING

WHEN old man Billie Bob Russell got ready to lay the steel down on his Yellow Dog railroad he sent for all the niggers for a hundred miles around.

"I'm laying down steel on the Yaller Dog line," he said. "From Yazoo City through the Delta. So what are you niggers going to do about that? I'm paying a dollar a day in camp and I want to hear that steel ring out. So get going, you bullies, and lay me down some steel. Old One-eyed Bill Shelly is going to pull the tail on the first train down the line, so I'm using ninety pound steel on white-oak cross-ties and nine-inch spikes to hold it down. So line out, you bullies, and lay me down some steel. Grab your hammers and let that steel ring out like a bell."

So the niggers got their shovels and buried the cross-ties. Then they got their hooks and they placed the steel end to end for a solid thousand miles. And then they got their hammers!

"Hold dem spikes, you holders," said the hammer men, "whilst I sinks dis spike in dat hard oak cross-tie." And they swung their hammers.

But the wood was hard and the spikes were long and they couldn't hide them in the ties. So the drivers made up a song and sang it to the holders and the holders listened and sang it back to them, line for line:

> "Dis old hammer—wham!
> Dis old hammer—wham!
> Jest a little too heavy—wham!
> Jest a little too heavy—wham!
> For my size—wham!
> Baby for my size—wham!"

"Drive 'em down, you bullies," said old man Billie Bob Russell. "Break the handle off, but bury them spikes in that white-oak tie."

So the drivers swung their hammers harder and they made up another song:

> "Hammer on, bullies—wham!
> Hammer on, bullies—wham!

And make yo' time—wham!
And make yo' time—wham!
'Cause I'm burnt out—wham!
'Cause I'm burnt out—wham!
And I can't make mine—wham!
Lawdy, and I can't make mine—wham!"

But there was a big nigger named Sam who wouldn't work with the others and he wouldn't sing with the others. He had his holder at the other end of the rail and he swung his hammer from his hip so hard that in just two licks he'd bury a nine-inch spike in white oak cross-ties.

"Sing, you niggers," Sam told them, "and bear down on dem spikes. But don't git in de way of a hammer-swingin' man like me, 'cause I'm burnin' out my holder jest holdin' de spikes for me to hit. Now watch me whilst I sings y'all a song and sinks more spikes den my holder kin hold." So he and his holder sang:

"Ain't no hammer—wham!
In dis Delta—wham!
Ring like mine—wham!
Lawdy, ring like mine—wham!
'Cause dis old hammer—wham!
Shine like silver—wham!

[142]

RING, STEEL, RING

And she ring like gold—wham!
Lawdy, ring like gold—wham!"

"Well, all right, Sam," said old man Billie Bob Russell. "You are a hammer-swinging man and you make it ring. So lay down on that handle and sink them nine-inch spikes. If you run out of spikes I'll haul you some more."

"I reckon hit ain't nobody kin handle a hammer like me," said Sam. "I comes f'm Georgia whar de hammer is a man's middle name. I was riz up wid a hammer handle to play wid over in Cobb County whar de marble comes f'm, and I reckon swingin' a hammer comes natchel for me. O' course I ain't de best hammer man in de world, but de best'n is daid now, so dat leave only me."

"Who say de best hammer man is daid?" It was Big John Henry that had come to camp, and he was six feet tall the day he got there. "I ain't daid, and I ain't f'm Georgia," said John Henry, "and I wan't bawn wid no hammer in my hand. But I comes f'm de Black River country whar hit's night all de time, and my feets don't tetch de ground. So I rousts and I roams and I rambles around, and I hauls my woman wid me. Whilst

I'm workin' on dis Yaller Dog line, she gonter cook my victuals. But efn hit's a man which kin drive more steel den me, well go and claim my victuals, 'cause my Julie Anne done told me, she say, 'John Henry, you's a man and I loves you good. But do I find a better man den you, well, git yo' hat and wawkin' cane and git on down de road.' So hyar I stand, full six foot tall and my feets don't tetch de ground. Yonder in de tent is my Julie Anne, cookin' turnip greens and cawnbread. So line up to de rail, you fat-mouf Sam, and le's see you swing yo' hammer. Efn you kin outswing me, den I don't want no supper."

"You's big and stout," said this nigger named Sam, "but you can't swing no hammer. You ain't big enough to hold de spikes whilst I sinks 'em in de cross-ties. But I ain't et no turnip greens and good old hard hoecake in so long dat I don't know when, and so I'm gonter race you.

"We'll jest drive spikes for a solid mile, and de man which wins gits de supper."

"Gimme a hammer," said John Henry, "and gimme two spike holders. I wants my hammer to weigh nine pounds and a handle er second-growth hickory. Slim and limber so she'll spring when I lays my strenk behind hit. And gimme some holders which sets and gits, so's I won't mash they hands off. So scatter down de track, you holders, and set spikes on dem cross-ties, 'cause I'm comin' down like I don't know what and old hell can't stop me."

All the holders lined up down the track, holding spikes on the cross-ties, and then Sam and John Henry got their hammers and lined up at the mark.

"I'll drop my hat," said old man Billie Bob Russell, "and when it hits the ground I want to hear them hammers ring and I want to see the spikes sink. We're laying a thousand miles of railroad line and we ain't hardly started. So line up, you hammer-swinging bullies, and set them spikes, you holders, because I'm fixing to drop my hat and start this thing a-going."

And then old man Billie Bob Russell's hat hit the ground. And when his hat hit the ground, the hammers rang like a bell! Every time Sam sank a spike, John Henry sank one, too, and every time John Henry sank a spike, old Sam swung his hammer. Down the track they went, sinking spikes at every lick and yelling for more room to work in. Sam worked faster, but John

JOHN HENRY

Henry worked harder. Sam sang him a song that
was as fast as his swinging:

> "Dis old hammer—wham!
> Killed John Henry—wham!
> But hit can't kill me—wham!
> Lawd, hit can't kill me—wham!"

But John Henry swung his hammer from his
hip like a song he knew and the words rolled out
with the swinging:

> "You hyar my nine-pound hammer ring,
> Oh, she ring jest like a bell.
> Don't let my hammer fall on you,
> 'Cause hit'll drive you plum to hell, Lawd, Lawd,
> And I tell you fare thee well."

John Henry and Sam stayed side by side for a
long time. John Henry sang and swung from his
hip, but finally Sam's eyes got a far-away look
and he changed his song to a new one:

> "Blow yo' whistle—wham!
> Mamma, you kin toot yo' hawn—wham!
> But when de Cap'm call me—wham!
> He'll find his driver gone—wham!"

And then old Sam burned out on the job! He staggered to the shade and yelled for the waterboy. "Take off my shoes," he said, "and open up my shirt at de neck, 'cause I seed de devil's pitchfawk."

So they took off his shoes and opened up his shirt, but John Henry kept on swinging.

"Go on, John Henry," said old man Billie Bob Russell. "You're a hammer-swinging man from I don't know where, and I like to hear that steel ring."

"Jes gittin' soople," John Henry said, "and jest gittin' started to sweatin'. So string out some more spike-holders down de line and bring me a brand-new hammer, 'cause I see de sun gittin' low in de west and I got to git done before sundown."

So they brought him a new hammer and they set his spikes, and all the holders sang a song for him to work by:

> "John Henry was a hammer-swingin' man,
>   Burned out dat nigger name' Sam.
> And ef dat ain't swingin' like a natchal man,
>   Well, den, I'll be damn, Lawd, Lawd,
>   Well, den, I'll be damn."

JOHN HENRY

John Henry swung his hammer until the sun went down, and when the sun went down he drove his last spike in that railroad line. So he said: "Well, I'm a man and I works like a man, so now I'm fixin' to eat. So go tell my woman to take de kittle offn de stove and go spread out my victuals. Pile my turnip greens tree-top tall and bury 'em down wid middlin'. Pour my pot-licker in a ba'l and bring my bread in a basket."

So John Henry went on back to camp and he walked up to his tent. "Whar my supper, baby?" he said. "Come on and feed John Henry."

But there wasn't a sound came from the tent, and John Henry looked about him.

So about that time the old woman came up and said, "Hit ain't no supper, John Henry. Yo' gal fed hit all to a nigger name' Sam, and den she got her bundle. And de last I seed er yo' Julie Anne she was cuttin' down de levee, swingin' on to old Sam's arm and gigglin' like she loved him."

So John Henry sat down on the ground and he looked at the old woman. "Ain't I a man?" he said. "And ain't I makin' her wages? Didn't I burn dat Sam out and didn't I swing my ham-

mer? How come dat woman quit a man like me
and take up wid dat fat-mouf?"

The old woman looked at John Henry and
then she looked at the moon. John Henry was
big and dark, but the moon was new and yellow.

"Ah, Lawd, John Henry," the old woman said.
"Ah, Lawd, John Henry. Efn I told you how
come Julie Anne left you, den you'd know mo'n
I know, 'cause Julie Anne is a woman and you's
a man. But, son, dat ain't de answer. You works
hard when Sam lays around, so Julie Anne up
and quit you. But dat ain't de reason, too, John
Henry, 'cause hit's jest de way things like dat
goes, and hit ain't no reason for hit. Sometime a
woman stick to a man, and sometime she up and
quit him. She do or she don't, 'cordin' to how
things is, but dat ain't de reason. So, ah, Lawd,
son," the old woman said. "Ah, Lawd, John
Henry. You's big and fine and six foot tall. Ah,
Lawd, John Henry."

DOWN THE ROAD

A MAN is a man and John Henry was six feet tall, but Julie Anne quit him for a nigger named Sam who wasn't half the man John Henry was. So the big man from the Black River country stood up by the side of his cook stove and he looked into the kettles. He had brought Julie Anne to the Yellow Dog camp to cook his victuals while he worked out on the railroad swinging a nine-pound hammer. But the stove was cold and the kettles were empty and Julie Anne was long gone.

"A woman," said John Henry, "is a heap er fun, but she kin be a heap er bother, too. So I'm a man which don't grieve after no woman when she's gone 'cause hit's more whar she comed f'm." And then he sang himself a song:

DOWN THE ROAD

"I was bawn in de Black River country
Twice as big as I kin be.
But hit ain't never yit been no woman
Kin make a fat-mouf outn me, Lawd, Lawd,
Kin make a fat-mouf outn me."

No sooner had John Henry sung that song until a girl named Ruby walked up. Ruby lived in a tent at the end of the line, but she had had her eye on big John Henry ever since he came into camp. So she said, "Listen at dat big old hammer-swingin' man sing dat fool song! Hit ain't no man on dis Delta kin swing a hammer like you and hit ain't no man nowhars kin sing a song like you. I told my sister, quick as I saw you, I says, 'Look at dat big old gi'nt,' I say, 'I bet dat big scound'el could change my mind all over de place, did he ha'fway try.'"

"Say which?" said John Henry.

"Say I told my sister, I say, 'Look at dat puny little old gal he brang along to take up wid'. I told her, I say, 'Dat Julie Anne ain't no kind er gal for a big hammer-swingin' man like John Henry.'"

"You was right," John Henry told Ruby. "Julie Anne wa'n't woman enough for a man like me, and neither is no yuther woman, 'cause

JOHN HENRY

I'm a man er my own and I does my work and I eats my victuals in de grub-shack, 'cause me and de gals don't git along and hit's too much trouble to bother. Gimme a nine-pound hammer wid a limber handle, or gimme a big cotton hook, or maybe a Number Four shovel, and I kin git along. But a woman wearies my mind and I don't like to bother. So git along, you Ruby gal, and make yo' tawk to some man which loves you, 'cause I'm done wid de ladies f'm now on, and I don't need no company."

So John Henry went to work on the line all day long, swinging his hammer and driving down spikes. He burned out all the other hammer-swinging men and then he started burning out the holders. " 'Cause I'm big and stout and my mind is free, and I eats my grub in de cook-tent. Ain't no weary woman on my mind and my soul don't bear no burden. So bring me a brand-new nine-pound sludge wid a four-foot hickory handle, and stand back, you bullies, 'cause I'm big and I'm named John Henry."

John Henry worked and sweated and ate, but he didn't have much fun and the cook-shack grub didn't suit his taste. So he went up to the old woman and asked her, he said: "How come

I ain't happy? I burned out all de mens on de job and about burned out de holders. I eats like a hog and I sleeps like a dog, but I don't feel so happy. So come on, old woman, and spread de news and tell me what de trouble."

The old woman took John Henry by the right hand and led him down the line. "You's a man," she said, "and you works like a man, and you think dat makes you happy. But, John Henry, you made yo' path, so you might jest as well put yo' foot in hit and wawk. Give you a cotton hook or a nine-pound sludge and ain't nobody kin fool you. Let de sun shine hot so's you kin sweat and you kin burn out de devil. But work ain't all a man got to do, 'cause a man got to have him a woman."

John Henry left the old woman and walked up and down the line all night long. The moon went down and the stars came out and the varmints in the bottoms sang and fought the whole night through while John Henry walked with his worry.

But when the sun came up John Henry went to Ruby's tent and called out to her: "Ruby," he told her, "ain't I a man, and can't I swing a hammer?"

[153]

JOHN HENRY

"You is and you kin, you big old gi'nt," Ruby told him.

"But a man got to eat," John Henry said.

"Ain't hit de trufe," Ruby said, "but how do you know? 'Cause ain't nobody ever fed a man like you like you ought to be eatin'. A man like you needs turnip greens so high you can't tetch bottom, wid middlin' meat b'iled down so soft hit slips down widout chewin'. And a heap er cabbages, too, wid a great big slugs er side meat. And den I dreens de potlicker off in a ba'l and feeds you dat wid a dipper. And I cooks cawn-bread in a four-foot pan and pour cracklin's in wid a shovel, 'cause a man like you got to eat like a man, and dat's how I'm gonter feed you. So step inside and take my right hand whilst I gits you up some breakfast, and whilst you's burnin' de hammer men down I'm gonter come out and watch you."

So John Henry took Ruby by the right hand and went into her tent for breakfast. Then he got a brand-new hammer and went to work out on the railroad. "Hold my spikes," he told the holders. "Set 'em and git, 'cause I'm comin'. I sinks a spike wid every lick, and I makes my hammer rattle. Set dem spikes on both sides er de rail, and don't let me see my shadow, 'cause I comes f'm de place whar de sun don't shine and I got to sweat down my breakfast."

So John Henry worked for forty days, and Ruby didn't let him get hungry. The harder he worked the more he ate and the more he ate the harder he worked, but always there was something missing. He talked and he bragged and he drove his spikes, but inside he was restless. Ruby fed him like a baby, and when she wasn't cooking for him in the tent, she came out to the railroad and watched while John Henry burned out the men, and then she would give them the yi-yi.

"Whyn't you be a man like my John Henry?" she yi-yied as the men hit the shade. "Look at dat big old gi'nt swing dat sludge and watch dem spikes sink down. 'Cause he's a man and he works like a man and you ought to see him ruin my victuals."

"Dat's de kind er woman for a man to have," the drivers told the holders. "No wonder John Henry kin lay us in de shade when he got a gal like Ruby. She feeds him so good dat he's fat and slick, and den she roots whilst he's workin'. I wisht I had me a gal like her, and den maybe I c'd do better."

JOHN HENRY

John Henry worked and ate like a fool, but he kept on feeling restless. "I wonder whar at is dat Julie Anne," he said, "and what she doin'. She ain't nothin' but a woman to me and I hope she livin' happy, but I wisht I knowed whar she gone off to and I wonder how come she quit me."

But he made the question one rainy night and nobody but the wet clouds heard it. Ruby was asleep and she didn't hear, and if she had she couldn't have answered. But John Henry wanted to know and he kept on seeking the answer. He couldn't find the answer in his work, and he couldn't find it in Ruby. So one day he told her to get him his hat and get him his walking-shoes.

" 'Cause maybe I got a eetch on my heel," he said, "or else I'm woman weary. Whatever hit is, I'm gittin' around and I'm travelin' by my lonesome. So fare you well, my Ruby gal, and keep yo' kittle b'ilin', 'cause hit's many a man like de way you cooks and you don't has to git lonesome."

"Fare you well," she told him, "and I wish you mighty well. But befo' you leave me you might tell me how come you's leavin'. And you might tell yo' Ruby, too, which way yo' toes is p'intin', 'cause I loves you sweet, you great big man, and I works so hard to please you."

So John Henry took Ruby by the right hand for the last time and he led her out of the tent. "Look at dat moon," he told her, "and look at dat ring around hit."

"What do dat mean?" she asked him.

"Hit mean de same thing which is why I'm leavin' you behind, gal," he said, "and hit got de answer whar I'm goin'."

"Don't ju-ju tawk me, darlin'," Ruby said. "Ain't I cooked for you since you been hyar? And ain't I fed you plenty? Ain't I mended yo' overhalls and ain't I treated you handsome? So don't ju-ju tawk at me; jest tell me what de moon say."

"Dat's de p'int," said John Henry. "You good to me and I loves you good, but now I'm fixin' to quit you. De answer is yonder up in de moon, and I wished I knowed de answer. De moon got a ring around his tail, and I'm all set for travelin'. Sometime de moon don't got a ring and sometime hit's all rung up. Sometime I ain't got no eetchin' heel, and sometime I got de run-arounds all over. Hit all one and de same, baby, so fare you well, my Ruby. Keep yo' cabbages b'iled down low, and keep yo' skillet greasy, 'cause hit's many a man love a gal like you, but as for me, I'm travelin'."

And John Henry took his hat and his walking-cane and he walked away from his sweet Ruby at the Yellow Dog railroad camp. He didn't know where he was bound for and he didn't know why he was leaving. But he had an itching heel and a run-around soul, because Julie Anne kept calling.

THE WAY WITH WOMEN

JOHN HENRY walked away from the Yellow
Dog railroad camp with his hat in his hand
and his head held high. He was looking at
the tree-tops and at the sun in the sky. In his
heart he was singing a farewell song to the
Yellow Dog and the Delta. " 'Cause I'm a man
and I works, and den I gits around," he said.
"I done worked and now hit's time to git around.
And dat's how come I'm travelin'." So he
opened up his mouth so the song in his heart
could sing out to the tree-tops as he got on
down the road:

"I works and I rambles and I rambles and works,
    And dat's de way I gits all around.

JOHN HENRY

I'm a natchal man and I'm six foot tall,
   And my feets don't tetch de ground, Lawd, Lawd,
   And my feets don't tetch de ground."

He didn't know where he was going and he didn't know what he was going for after he got there, but the strange gravel on the new road scratched his itching heel, and that was all he wanted to know.

But the first thing he knew he came up to a landing on the river, and about that time he looked up and saw the *Big Jim White* with her wheels churning water and her nose pointed toward the bank. The captain was standing on the hurricane deck, cursing and yelling, and the mate was on the boiler deck, relaying it down. And the driver was on the main deck, filling in the gaps left by the captain and mate. The whistle was blowing and the bell was ringing and the winch was screeching as the stage came down.

"I bet dat boat is fixin' to land hyar," said John Henry. "And I bet dey needs a rouster to load on all dis cotton, 'cause how dey gonter git dis cotton down he plank efn dey ain't got plenty er rousters? And hit ain't no man kin roust like me, and ev'ybody knows hit."

Then John Henry put his hands up to his mouth and roared like a frog in the canebrake: "Hey, you nigger wid de landin'-line! Chunk me dat rope you got in yo' hand. I'm gonter tie down de *Big Jim White* so's us kin load dis cotton."

Then John Henry grabbed the headlines and dragged the *Big Jim White* in and tied her to a cypress tree. And before the stage hit the ground that big man from the Black River country had a bale of cotton rolling.

"Gimme dat cotton, you niggers," the driver yelled. "And efn y'all can't roust hit, well, gangway for a man which can, for yonder stands John Henry!"

"Efn you can't see a man my size," John Henry told the driver, "jest watch de way dis cotton rolls, and tell me what my name is."

The rousters stood back while John Henry rolled the cotton; and while John Henry rolled cotton the rousters sang:

"John Henry was a cotton-rollin' man.
   He had his hook in his hand all de time.
And befo' he'd let de driver burn him down,
   I bet he'd die wid his hook in his hand, Lawd, Lawd,
   And he rousts like a natchal man."

[161]

JOHN HENRY

When the boat was loaded and the gangplank raised John Henry went on deck and sat down on top of the cotton. All the other rousters lay around and talked about the good times down the river and what they were going to do when they got to New Orleans. But John Henry just listened.

Finally a big rouster named Sam turned to John Henry and asked him, he said, "What you aimin' to do when you gits down de river?"

"Who, me?" said John Henry.

"Do yo' foot fit a limb?" said Sam.

"Wait to I gits down de river," John Henry said, "and den I'll make up my mind. But I hyars hit's a heap er grub and a heap er ladies over back er town."

When the rousters heard that they laughed. "Maybe you didn't make up yo' mind," they said, "when you was totin' three sacks er sugar on de up-trip hunh? Maybe you didn't make up you' mind when you was sweetin' dat Julie Anne gal around de boat, hunh? Maybe you jest worked like a dog so's she could ride because you was waitin' to git up de river to make up yo' mind?

THE WAY WITH WOMEN

That made John Henry mad! He stood up on a bale of cotton and roared so loud that the boat stood still. He roared again and it started backing up. And he roared one more time and the river shook between the levees.

"Don't make me mad," John Henry said, and he grabbed the rouster named Sam and flung him in the river. "Don't make me mad," he said again, and he picked up a bale of cotton and threw it at the other rousters, " 'Cause dat Julie Anne ain't none er mine and I long since give her de go-by."

The rousters kept quiet after that, but John Henry was not happy. He sat and simmered inside his soul until finally he couldn't stand it. "Julie Anne wa'n't no woman er mine," he told the other rousters. "I had a gal in de Yaller Dog camp which tuck and cooked my victuals. A big, long-legged gal, slick and black, which I called Ruby. Now Ruby was de gal for me, and, Lawd, how dat gal cooked victuals!"

He shut his eyes and saw his tent in the Delta country, with Ruby cooking at the stove and calling for her darling. "Turnip greens stacked up tree-top high and cabbages cooked wit middlin'! And cawnpone cooked in a four-foot pan all loaded down wid cracklin's!"

But while he had his eyes shut, watching Ruby cook all the grub, he saw a big stranger walk in her tent and stick his feet under the table!

"Un-uhn!" said John Henry. "Hit must er been some changes made since I left de Delta." Then he opened his eyes and looked at the river, and then he looked at the willows on the levee. "I don't love dat Ruby gal," he said. "I jest loved her cookin'."

The boat rocked on down the river and John Henry kept on thinking. He'd close his eye and try to see what lay before him, but the best he could see was a misty fog and the sound of many voices. So finally the old driver came up and told him, he said: "John Henry, you looks wearied. De last time I seed you, you was haulin' a gal, and now you's travelin' lonesome. Whar at is dat Julie Anne which you hauled up de river?"

"God knows," John Henry said, " 'cause one day when I was workin' she tuck up wid a nigger name' Sam, and dat's de last I seed er dat gal."

"John Henry," the driver said, "when hit comes to roustin' you can't be beat, and I hyars you swings a hammer, but you ain't much around de gals, so why don't you give 'em de go-by?"

"Who ain't much around de gals?" John Henry asked. "Man, I kin git more women den I kin handle, and dat's sayin' a heap. I had Ruby and Delia and Julie Anne, and I up and quit Poor Selma. I gits me a woman and den I quits, and den I gits me another."

"You might er quit Poor Selma," said the driver, "but Julie Anne quit you, 'cause I kin see you grievin' in yo' heart, and you know dat's de natchal."

"Julie Anne quit me," John Henry said, "but I was mighty good to her."

"Sho," said the driver. "Dat's de way dey'll do you ev'y time. You do for a woman and she do you bad. But you treat 'em hard and make 'em work, and dey love you good."

"Dat might be right," said John Henry, " 'cause I didn't do for Ruby, and she done for me, rain or shine, and she hung her haid when I quit her."

"Well," said the driver, "hit ain't no need in argyin', 'cause a woman is a woman, no matter whar, and dat de way you got to treat 'em. You kin handle a cotton hook, and I hyars you kin

[165]

swing a hammer. But you got to handle a woman hard, or else you got some trouble."

John Henry closed his eyes once more and looked down the river. The *Big Jim White* was churning away, eating up the distance. So he stood up and roared like a lion, and all the rousters listened.

"Swarm around me, you river rats, and listen," John Henry told them. "When I gits down de river I'm gonter git my woman. She's settin' in de parlor, cryin' for me and wishin' I was wid her. So I'll take my wages and buy her some clothes and git her dressed up purty. And den I'll strut by her warm side so's all er y'all kin see me. I knows how to handle cotton and I knows how to swing a hammer, but de best thing I knows is how to treat de ladies and how to make 'em love me. I does for her and she do me bad, but dat don't bile no cabbage, 'cause a gal ain't stiddy in her haid and she liable to git foolish. So git out er my way, you rousters, and watch old John Henry, 'cause I'm big and bad and I'm six foot tall and I makes my woman love me."

Then John Henry stood up and did a dance on top of the cotton that shook the boat. Then he opened up his mouth and sang a song:

THE WAY WITH WOMEN

"My Julie Anne, she went away f'm me,
  But I knowed whar she was at.
So I got out my shoes and my wawkin'-cane,
  And I put on my Stutson hat, Lawd, Lawd,
  And I put on my Stutson hat."

DOING FOR HIS WOMAN

WHEN John Henry got to New Orleans he went straight to Saratoga Street, where he knew he would find his Julie Anne. She was sitting on the doorstep, crying, and the nigger named Sam was standing on the banquette, abusing her.

"I'm sick and tired er yo' blubberin' and gwine on," Sam told her. "You ain't done nothin' but tell me how stout dat John Henry is and den set down and cry ev'y since I been keepin' company wid you. Now you hysh up dat blubberin'. You hyar?"

"I can't stop," Julie Anne said, " 'cause I miss my John Henry so bad."

"Well den, I'm gonter give you somethin' to blubber about," Sam said. "I'm gonter haul off and smack you down. Dat's what I'm gonter do to you." And he raised his hand like he was fixing to hit Julie Anne.

But he never hit her. John Henry hit Sam first and knocked him clear across the street. "Now mind out, Sam," John Henry told him. "Don't make me mad or I'll come over and hit you. You jest drag on down de street and leave dis woman be. You hyar me?"

So Sam went off, and John Henry stepped up and took Julie Anne by the right hand and said, "I'm glad to see you, darlin'."

Julie Anne quit crying and she held John Henry's big hand in both of hers. "Me, too," she said. "I knowed you'd hunt me up and come and git me. I never did love no man but you, but I got so lonesome in dat Yaller Dog camp, darlin', I'd a run off wid a mule efn he had pants on."

"Dat's all right," John Henry said. "I ain't got no hard feelin's. I'm too glad to git back to you to stand hyar and argy."

"Well, efn dat's de way you feels," said Julie Anne, "go hang yo' hat on de hatrack."

John Henry went inside and hung up his hat. Then he sat down and took off his shoes and threw them under the bed. Then Julie Anne came in, happy and smiling. "I sho am glad you come back home," she said to John Henry.

"Me, too," John Henry said, and his heart was bursting with joy. But before he knew what he was doing he stood up and slapped Julie Anne down on the floor. And when he did that a big ache came over his soul and a tear drained from his eye.

"I didn't aim to do dat, sweet," he told her. "I didn't know I was gonter hit you and I don't know how come I did. I jest th'owed out my hand and hit smacked you down. I'm too sorry, darlin'."

Then he stooped down and picked Julie Anne up and stood her on her feet. "I'm too sorry," he said again. "I didn't want to hit you."

Julie Anne smiled and brushed his face with her hands, "Dat's all right, darlin'," she told him. "I ain't got no hard feelin's about dat. And hit didn't hurt so awful."

Then John Henry slapped her down again, and again tears drained from his eyes when he saw his poor little Julie Anne in a heap on the floor. She was crying low down in her throat and looking at John Henry.

DOING FOR HIS WOMAN

"No mind me, darlin'," she said. "Dat slappin' didn't hurt so much, and I guess I had hit comin'."

But John Henry couldn't say a word. His heart was dripping sorrow for having slapped his woman. He had never done anything like that before and he didn't know why he did that.

"Julie Anne, darlin'," he said, "I didn't aim to slap you. I don't know how come I did, but hit sho hurt my feelin's. Maybe I got too much troubles on my mind, and maybe I better git goin', 'cause I'd druther lose my big right arm den to hurt you jest a little."

And John Henry got his hat and walked up and down the street. There were a heap of houses along the street and a heap of people walking on the sidewalks. But they all whirled around before John Henry and he couldn't tell which was where, so he kept right on walking.

Finally he came up to that nigger named Sam, and he grabbed him by the collar. "Looky hyar, Sam," he said, "hit's good dat you didn't hurt my woman."

Then he knocked Sam down again, and kept right on walking.

After a while he came up with old Blind

Lemon, sitting on the corner playing his guitar
and singing his one-line song:

"I love you, woman, but I don't like yo' low-down ways."

John Henry stopped and listened awhile and
Blind Lemon kept right on singing that same old
one-line song. So finally John Henry asked him,
he said: "Lemon, whyn't you go on and finish
dat song. Hit sound good while hit's goin', but
hit ain't got nowhars. Come on and sing me de
rest er dat song."

Blind Lemon stopped singing and looked at
John Henry. "Ain't dat enough?" he asked him.
"Son, listen at old Blind Lemon, 'cause I'm gonter tell you somethin' you don't know, 'cause
don't nobody know onless he's been dar, and efn
he been dar, hit ain't no good in me tellin'. Efn
you love a woman but you don't like her low-
down ways, den you got trouble to last you all
er yo' days."

John Henry took Blind Lemon by the right
hand. "You might be blind and can't see," he
told him, "but you sho kin see inside er my poor
heart, 'cause I loves a gal, but she sho treat me
low down. I do for her and she do me bad."

DOING FOR HIS WOMAN

Blind Lemon took John Henry by the right hand and told him, he said: "Son, dat's trouble you got. Pyore trouble. And de doctor can't do you no good. You got a trouble which gonter plague you so long as you's in yo' right mind. Some fo'ks tries to smother hit down wid cocaine, and some tries to drown hit in gin. But de trouble is on you, son, long as you loves dat gal." Then Blind Lemon sang John Henry one more song:

> "Take a shot er cocaine,
> And take a shot er gin.
> You kin tell hit'll kill yo' troubles,
> But you can't tell when.

"And," said Blind Lemon, "don't nobody keer when efn he got a triflin' woman on his mind, 'cause hit ain't but one thing gonter ease dat trouble, son, and dat's when you fold up and die."

John Henry knew Blind Lemon was telling him the natural truth, so he walked down the street with a heavy heart and a soul like solid lead. But he held his head up and sang a weary, lonesome song:

JOHN HENRY

"I loves me a friv'lin woman,
   And her name is Julie Anne.
She treat me like a dirdy dog,
   But I do's be best I kin, Lawd, Lawd,
   And I do's de best any man kin."

About that time John Henry came up with Old Aunt Dinah. She was sitting on her doorstep, looking up and down the street.

"Hey, John Henry," she said, "I hyar you singin' a song, but hit sound like a sad-heart song. Hit's a mighty nice day to be singin' such a droopy song."

"Dat wa'n't me singin', Old Aunt Dinah," John Henry told her. "Dat was a burden on my heart which you hyared singin', 'cause I got troubles. Efn I didn't had no troubles I'd be singin' me a glad song. But, naw, I got de down-yonders so bad in my heart dat hit thump like a chunk er lead in my bosom."

Old Aunt Dinah didn't say a word. She took John Henry by the right hand and sang him a song:

"I'm gonter make my troubles easy,
   On my knees.
I'm gonter make my troubles easy,
   On my knees.

DOING FOR HIS WOMAN

I'm gonter git down on my knees
And say, Jesus, he'p me, please.
I'm gonter make my troubles easy,
    On my knees."

"Well," said John Henry, "my troubles bearin'
down mighty hard, but hit ain't got me down
on my knees yit. I kin tote a five-hund'ed pound
bale er cotton on my back, and I kin swing a
nine-pound hammer to she ring like a bell. And
I sho ain't gonter let no runty little old gal like
Julie Anne put me on my knees."

"You tawks might' brash," Old Aunt Dinah
told him. "Dat might sound like man tawk to
you, but hit sound like fool tawk to me."

"Hit might sound like man tawk," John
Henry said, "and hit might sound like fool tawk.
But hit sho was a man which said hit, 'cause I'm
six foot tall and I works like a dog, and hit ain't
no man kin shade me. I'm big and bad and I
rambles and roams, and my feets don't tetch de
ground, 'cause I comes f'm de Black River country whar de sun don't never shine. So fare you
well, Aunt Dinah."

Then John Henry went back to the house
and found Julie Anne on the doorstep with a

tear in her eye, but she smiled sweet when she saw him. "I'm sho glad you comed back home," she said, " 'cause I was lonesome."

"Did you miss me whilst I was gone?" John Henry asked her.

"I sho did, darlin'," she said.

But John Henry went through the house and he saw a man's tracks leading from his back door step to the alley!

"Looky hyar, gal," he said, "who made dem tracks?"

"Which tracks?" she asked him.

"You kin see dem tracks, same as me," he said. "Who been creepin'?"

Julie Anne looked at the tracks and then she looked up and down the street. Then she cried and told John Henry. "Hit's a friend of mine name' Sam," she said, "comed hyar whilst you was ramblin'. But I won't never let him come no more efn you say you don't want him."

"I don't keer how much he comes," said John Henry, " 'cause I'm leavin' you hyar and now, and you kin have dat nigger."

Julie Anne cried and begged John Henry to stay. " 'Cause," she said, "no matter what I done you knows I'm yo' woman. I can't change dat and neither kin you, nor neither kin Sam or de doctor. You know I'm yo's and you know you's mine. So set down and stay, John Henry."

John Henry looked at Sam's tracks and then he looked at Julie Anne. "Well," he said, "don't let him come no more, and keep de back door bolted, 'cause you do's me bad but I love you good. Now go and git yo' bonnet, 'cause I'm gonter dress you up purty. I'll buy you a dress and a great big hat and high-heel shoes and stockin's. So come on, darlin', whilst I buys you some clothes, 'cause dat's how good I loves you."

THE HOW LONG SONG

JOHN HENRY spent all his money on fine clothes for his woman and then he got his overalls and struck out for the river. He found the driver of the *Big Jim White* and asked for a job of rousting.

"I'm f'm de Black River country," John Henry said, "and hit ain't no man a-livin' which kin outroust me. I totes my cotton hook in my hand, or I kin roust off sugar. I needs to work to make some wages, 'cause I done dressed up my woman.

"I buyed her a solid red silk dress and socks and high-heel slippers. I buyed her some green-and-gold year bobs and a great big four-bit diamond. And den I buyed her a coal-black hat as big as all-git-out wid a snow-white dove settin' on one side to hold dat fool thing on her.

THE HOW LONG SONG

And, man, when dat woman wawks down de street you ought to see her struttin'. Wid big old me wawkin' by her warm side in my box coat and my John B. Stutson!"

"You doin' for dat gal again?" the driver asked John Henry. "And she still treatin' you like a dog, or else I don't know women."

"Dat gal told me she love me true," John Henry told the driver. "And how kin she he'p hit when I puts de true love on her soul and spends my money on her, 'cause ain't I a man? I'm big and stout and dey don't come no better."

"Git in line," the driver said. "De more you works de better you's off. So grab a bale er cotton."

John Henry took his big cotton hook in his right hand and started rolling cotton. The day was hot and he sweated big and his muscles worked like rubber. His heart was light because he felt so good and he knew his woman loved him.

"Git out er my way, you bullies," he said, "and don't git in de way er dis cotton, 'cause I'm a roustin' fool f'm I don't know whar, and old hell can't stop me. My woman is waitin' in a red silk dress, and moanin' for me to come home wid my pocket full er wages." Then he opened his mouth and sang himself a cotton-rolling song while he kept the bales rolling down the plank:

> "I'm big and black and I'm six foot tall,
>   And my feets don't tetch de ground.
> I'll roll dis cotton round and round
>   And I'll roll dis cotton down, Lawd, Lawd,
>   And I'll burn you rousters down."

When John Henry sang that song there was a nigger named Sam raised up and listened. Then Sam stuck his cotton hook in the ground and sang back at John Henry:

> "Well, I ain't hardly six foot tall
>   And my feet sticks in de ground.
> Cotton so heavy and de sun so hot,
>   To I b'lieve I'm burnin' down, Lawd, Lawd,
>   So I lays my cotton hook down."

"Well," said John Henry, "dat's jest one man I burned out, mighty nigh as quick as I started. And hit's a long time to sundown. So look out you bullies, or else I'll lay you all in de shade befo' de sun goes down, 'cause I'm f'm de Black River country whar de sun don't never shine and I don't git soople to de sun gits hot and my muscles don't work to somebody burns out, 'cause I'm so stout I don't know my strenk, and dis cotton can't show me."

John Henry rolled cotton until the sun went down, and he was just getting warmed up. "I wisht dat sun would come up again," he told the rousters, "so's I could git up a sho-nuff sweat whilst I'm rollin' cotton."

"I thought dat sun done hung in de sky," a rouster told John Henry. "I swear to my soul I was burnin' down, and I'm sho glad I'm quittin'."

"Dat's 'cause you ain't stout like me," John Henry told the rouster. "Or maybe yo' woman ain't doin' you right and make you have woman-troubles, 'cause onless yo' heart is restin' easy, same as yo' muscles, you can't git no good licks at dis cotton."

"My woman doin' me all O. K.," the rouster said. "I keeps her too busy washin' clothes to git in any devilment. She ain't got no fancy dress and clothes to go out friv'lin'. Naw, hit ain't my woman which tires me out. Hit's cause I gits tired er workin'."

That made John Henry feel so good he got up and made his say-so. "Woman and work is all a man need, do he know how to handle 'em. Hit's some which can't handle work and hit's some which can't handle women. But dey hang around and drink dey gin and sniff up all de cocaine. But me, I kin work like I never been bawn, and when it comes to women, I got my Julie Anne all dressed up and waitin' for me to come home. She ain't so purty, but she love me so good, so I done made up a song I'm gonter sing y'all niggers:

> "Her eyes shine like diamonds,
>   And her teef shine about de same.
> Got a lip like a big slice er liver,
>   And hair like a hoss's mane, Lawd, Lawd,
>   And she love me jest de same.

"And dat," said John Henry, "is de natchal trufe."

"Man," said one of the rousters, "you must got you a woman. Efn I had a woman like dat, I'd be skeered to leave her alone 'cause I'm skeered some yuther nigger would change her mind and come creepin' whilst I'm gone."

John Henry laughed. "You might," he said, " 'cause you ain't big enough to make no woman love you like my gal love me. I kin go away and stay gone so long, and den I comes back home and th'ows my shoes under de bed jest like I ain't never been outn de house, 'cause all dat gal do is grieve after me when I'm gone."

Then John Henry put his wages in his pocket and went home. When he got to the house the front door was locked!

"How come my front door locked?" he said. "Whar my woman, and why ain't she settin' on de doorsteps waitin' for me to come home?"

And before anybody could answer that, a girl named Ruby, who lived right across the street, sang a song at John Henry:

"Been some changes made since you been gone.
　　Yeah, hit's been some changes made since you been gone.
　　Come home dis evenin' 'bout six o'clock,
　　You knock on de door and de door is locked.
　　So jest raise up de window and stick in yo' haid,
　　You'll find a great big stranger in yo' foldin'-bed.
　I say, hit's been some changes made since you been gone."

"Who you singin' at?" John Henry asked her.
"Do yo' foot fit a limb?" Ruby asked him. "Efn hit do, well, maybe you's a owl and kin holler 'who' all you want to."

But about that time Julie Anne unlocked the front door and let John Henry in. "I been sleepin'," she told him, "and dat Ruby gal make so much racket I shet de door to keep out de noise. Come on in, darlin', and hang up yo' hat in de hall. Hit ain't no supper cooked yit, but gimme yo' wages and I go over to de store and buy you some."

"How come hit ain't no supper cooked?" John Henry asked her. " 'Cause you know I been workin' hard and you know how hongry I gits when I'm workin'."

"I buys you a heap er supper, darlin'." she told him. "Sardine fish and potted ham and a great big box er crackers."

So John Henry hung his hat up, but he looked, and saw the back door open!

"How come de front door all locked up, and how come de back door open?"

"Was de back door open?" Julie Anne asked him.

John Henry walked to the back door and looked on the ground. Then he looked at Julie Anne. "Hit's some tracks leadin' out er de door, too," he said. "How come dat, woman?"

Julie Anne hung her head like a weeping willow. "John Henry," she said, "I ain't gonter lie, 'cause I loves you too good to fool you. Hit's a friend er mine name' Sam been hyar, and, darlin', I too sorry."

John Henry's heart turned into a solid rock. His shoulders drooped and his jaw dropped down, and he felt like all the cotton he had rolled all his life was piled upon his shoulders. He hung his head and looked at the ground, and then he looked at his woman. His voice was sad like a frog in the brake, and his words sounded like an old woman's: "I buyed you a dress and I buyed you a hat and I buyed you some high-heeled slippers. Den I rolled cotton to de sun went down and come home and give you my wages. And whilst I'm doin' all er dat you ain't got time to cook supper 'cause you too busy lockin' up de front door and friv'lin' wid dat creeper." He looked at the tracks in his back yard and then he looked at his woman. "I slapped you yistiddy," he said, "when hit hurt my soul. But now I ought to choke you."

Julie Anne looked at the tracks in the yard and then she looked at John Henry. Then she unbuttoned her dress at the neck and held her chin up. "Yeah," she said, "you ought to. So take my neck in yo' big hands and wring hit like a chicken's, 'cause I ain't no good and I done you wrong whilst you was out a-workin'. I know you don't love me no more, and so hit ain't no fun in livin'. So come on, darlin', and wring my neck, 'cause dat's all hit's good for."

But John Henry didn't touch her. Instead he stood and looked at his woman while the tears drained from his eyes. "Baby," he said, "maybe you's wrong, but hit don't make no diffunce. I loves you like I don't know what, and I ain't got de heart to tetch you. You's burned up my heart and you's pizened my soul, but somehow hit don't hurt me."

Then Julie Anne took him by his right hand and led him back to the room.

"Take off yo' shoes," she said, "and rest yo' feet whilst I cooks you some supper."

While John Henry took off his shoes and sat down to wait, Julie Anne cooked up turnip greens with middlin', and made cornbread in a four-foot pan and crammed it full of cracklin's. She boiled her cabbage with a side of meat and cooked his peas with hog jowl.

But when she finished cooking, John Henry

[186]

got up and got his hat, and left her in the kitchen.

"Come on, darlin'," Julie Anne said. "I got de kind er supper a big man like you likes so good after he been workin'."

But John Henry shook his head. "Nawp," he said, "I ain't hongry. I b'lieve I'll git out and git some air. My head feel kind er heavy."

And John Henry walked out of the house. Then Julie Anne went and locked the back door and sat on her front steps, crying and waiting.

NO REST FOR THE WEARY BURDEN

JOHN HENRY went out into the street and walked up and down. He was weary and tired and his soul bore down like lead. He was hungry and he didn't want to eat. He was thirsty and he didn't want to drink. He was lonesome and he didn't want to talk to anybody. So he walked along with his head held high, but he was talking to himself.

"I'm big and bad and six foot tall," he said, "but I got de all-overs all over me. I comes f'm de Black River country whar de sun don't never shine and I takes de shade for no man. I burned dat nigger name' Sam out and he crept right in my back door. I bought my Julie Anne some good-lookin' clothes and she treat me like a dog. I kin lift five hund'ed pounds er cotton at one lick and I kin sink a nine-inch spike in a white-oak tie. I kin fire for One-Eyed Bill Shelly and I kin roust a hog like he was a sack er meal. But I can't lift dat Julie Anne gal offn my poor soul. Ruby hung her head and cried when I quit her, and when I left Poor Selma she ain't never been de same. But Julie Anne bear down on my soul so bad."

About that time he came up on old Blind Lemon, sitting on the corner playing his guitar and singing his one-line song:

"I love you, woman, but I don't like yo' low-down ways."

"Dat de onliest song you sings, hunh?" said John Henry. "Hit speaks a natchal, but hit don't tell me nothin' to ease my weary mind."

"Hit's another song," said Blind Lemon, "but hit ain't my song."

"Le's hyar hit," said John Henry.

So Blind Lemon sang:

"Take a shot of cocaine,
    Take a shot er gin.
Know hit'll kill my troubles,
    But I don't know when."

"Will dat stuff kill yo' troubles?" John Henry asked him.

[189]

JOHN HENRY

"Hit ain't never kilt mine," said Blind Lemon. "De song say so, and I ain't de kind to argy wid no man's song. But hit ain't never eased mine."

So John Henry walked on down the street to Mink Eye's place and he went inside. There were a heap of people in there, drinking and jollying, and there were a heap of people sitting in the corners crying like their hearts were on the ground and their woman was stepping on them at every step. One old man got up and said, "I'm gonter sing y'all a song," and he did:

> "I'm old and rough
>   And skinny and tough
>   And I ain't never yit
>   Got drunk enough,
>   So baby don't you grieve after me."

Everybody laughed at that and he sat down. So about that time there was a girl named Ruby walked up to John Henry and took him by the hand. "Hello, Big Stuff!" she told him. "How about a little drink er gin wid me, hunh?"

"I works by myse'f," John Henry said, "and I drinks by myse'f when I drinks. And I ain't so sho I'm drinkin'."

"Livin' true to yo' darlin' gal?" Ruby asked him.

"Maybe so," said John Henry. "And den maybe I ain't got no darlin' gal."

"Maybe," said Ruby, "and den maybe you is."

"Maybe I is," said John Henry. "And maybe I ain't drinkin' wid you, 'cause you don't suit my style."

Ruby laughed. "You must not suit dat darlin' gal's style, or else you wouldn't be mopin' around like a chicken wid de mopes."

"Maybe," said John Henry.

"And," said Ruby, "maybe she got a footpath leadin' up to her back door, whilst you's mopin' around."

"Maybe," said John Henry, and he took Ruby by the right hand. "Le's go and git some gin," he said, " 'cause I got a grievin' in my heart."

So they went up and had a drink of gin.

"Dis stuff," said John Henry, "might be bad, but hit don't tetch me. Hit'll take mo'n dis dishwater to drown my weary pains."

"Maybe a little happy dust might he'p hit along," said Ruby.

"Maybe," said John Henry.

So Ruby whispered in Mink Eye's ear and he

gave them a paper with powders in it. "Hold dat to yo' nose and whiff," Ruby told John Henry. And he did as she told him.

"Hit ain't tetched me yit," John Henry said.

"Hit take time," Ruby told him. "You come and set down by me and let hit work."

"I wisht I'd 'a' been settin' down by a woman like you for so long," John Henry told her, "and den I wouldn't a had de down-yonders like I got."

"What you need," Ruby told him, "is a gal like me to make a fuss over you. Look at a big man like you, mopin' around 'cause some gal done you bad! What do dey call you, Big'n'?"

John Henry stood up and raised up his right arm. "John Henry is my name," he said, "and I'm six foot tall. I travels around like a ramblin' fool and hit ain't nobody kin shade me. I was bawn in de Black River country whar de sun don't never shine, and I kin handle my woman."

"You ain't John Henry sho 'nuff, is you, darlin'?" Ruby asked him. "Not de John Henry from de Black River country whar de sun don't never shine?"

"I ain't my brother," he said.

"Well, my name is Ruby," she told him, "and

I kin love a man like you. You big old scound'el, I bet you look good all dressed up like I'm gonter dress you up in a box coat and a John B. Stutson hat."

"I looks good in anything," John Henry told her, "'cause I'm big and bad and tree-top tall and my feet don't tetch de surface."

"Well, all right, den," said Ruby. "And I'm gonter dress you up like I don't know what, cause you's about my style."

"I likes you, Ruby," John Henry said, "and I likes de way you tawks. But hit's one thing I got on my mind, an dat's dat yuther woman."

"Humph!" said Ruby. "Forgit dat gal, 'cause she ain't doin' you right. I don't know what kind er gal she is onless she's jest pyore crazy.—Hyar, Mink Eye, bring us another whiff er dust, 'cause us is mighty friendly."

So John Henry took his cocaine in his left hand and he took Ruby's hand in his right hand, and he whiffed.

"Yeah," he said, "dat gal sho do me bad, but Lawd, Lawd, I love her."

"Don't tawk like dat," Ruby said. "Forgit dat gal which wrongs you. Think about me settin' hyar bustin' open wid lovin'."

JOHN HENRY

"She my Julie Anne," John Henry said, "and I'm sorry I slapped her. Maybe she was wrong and maybe she was right, but hit don't make no diffunce, 'cause she's my woman and I can't he'p dat, and I wonder what she's doin'."

He closed his eyes to look around and he saw the Black River country with the old woman making her charms with herbs in a copper kettle.

"Open up his eyes," the old woman said, "so's he kin see about him. He's a man in size and a man in strenk, but all he knows is workin'."

While he was watching the old woman make her charms he saw all the women he had ever known flying like bats around her. There was Ruby and Delia, and some he'd forgot, and there was Poor Selma, flapping their black rubbery wings and making screaming sounds at him.

Then suddenly into the group of girls came his little Julie Anne, all dressed up in white with wings like a dove, saying sweet words to him: "John Henry, darlin', you know how good I loves you. I waits for you when you rambles around and I'm always glad to see you. So put dat grievin' outn' yo' heart and come on home to me."

NO REST FOR THE WEARY BURDEN

But while she was telling John Henry that, he saw a big nigger named Sam come up and take her by the hand. She gave John Henry just one more smile and then went off with the creeper!

That made John Henry mad, and he jumped up and down on the table. "Don't make me mad," he said, "or else I'll bust dis place up!"

He grabbed up a chair and swung it around and knocked out all the lights. He threw the table at the men and threw chairs at the women. He tore off the roof and he tore up the floor, and then he tore down the walls. Then he walked out the door.

"I don't like dis kind er stuff," John Henry told Mink Eye. "Hit might be good for dem which does, but hit don't make me happy." So he grabbed Mink Eye and threw him across the street. "And now," he said, "I'm huntin' for Ruby. She sweet-tawked me when I was sad, and I sho aims to whup her."

But Ruby was long gone.

Then John Henry got on back home, feeling worse than ever. Julie Anne was on the doorstep, crying softly for him. "I knowed you'd come back," she said, "so I been waitin' up for you."

John Henry sat down and took her by the hand. "Baby," he said, "I been worried. I had a burden on my soul 'cause de way you been doin'. I don't know how come I grieve for you, 'cause I know you done quit friv'lin'. But I went to drown my burden wid happy dust and licker. But I seed all de women I ever knowed all rigged out like bullbats. All 'cept you, baby, and you looked like a snow-white dove and you was weepin' like a willow. But hit was a nigger name' Sam come tuck you away whilst you was sweet-tawkin' me."

"Dat was jest a bad dream," she told John Henry, "about dat Sam, 'cause I done quit him, jest like I told you."

John Henry was glad down in his heart. "But," he said, "I'm hungry. I didn't eat no supper tonight and I'm feelin' kind er empty. So go dish me up some turnip greens and cawn-bread wid cracklin's."

Julie Anne looked at the ground and then she looked up and down the street. "Nawp," she said, "hit's too late for dat."

"How come?" said John Henry. "Hit ain't

never too late for a man to eat when he gits hongry."

Julie Anne hung her head and cried, "Darlin'," she said to him, "I wouldn't tell you no lie, 'cause you knows I love you. But when you left dat nigger name' Sam come back, and so I fed him."

LORD, MY BURDEN

JOHN HENRY sat on the doorstep and he looked up and down the street. It was hot weather, but he wasn't working. His muscles felt stout and his back felt strong, but his weary heart ached like a pain and he wouldn't drive himself to his job. Inside the house Julie Anne was ironing clothes to make a dollar a day. But John Henry knew that there was a path leading out of the alley straight up to his back door.

"I don't know how come she weary me so bad," he said. "She ain't nothin' but a little nubbin of a woman, and she don't weigh hardly a hund'ed pounds. And me I kin put a five-hund'ed pound bale of cotton on my back and dog-trot down de gangplank."

Then Julie Anne sang a song over her ironing-board that showed John Henry where her mind was:

"Blow yo' whistle; papa you kin toot yo' hawn.
Blow yo' whistle; papa you kin toot yo' hawn.
Gonter wake up some mawnin' and find yo' mamma gone."

Julie Anne sang the song good and it sounded sweet in John Henry's ears, but it stuck in his soul like a cotton hook.

"Poor Selma was bigger den her," John Henry said, "and Ruby was twice as purty, but I swear to my soul dat woman wears me down."

So he shut his eyes and looked back to the Black River country where the sun don't never shine. He saw the old woman fussing around with her herbs and charms and laughing deep down in her stomach. But she wouldn't look at him. So he stood up and sang a song at the whole world:

"Work don't hurt no natchal man,
And I kin work, rain or shine.
But de way my Julie Anne do me bad
Eats out dis heart er mine, Lawd, Lawd,
Burns up dis soul er mine."

JOHN HENRY

Then the old woman looked at John Henry and said: "Hold up yo' haid and be a man, or bow yo' haid and die."

John Henry was a man and he held up his head. The way his woman treated him burned out his heart and ate up his soul, but nothing could get his rubber-like muscles and he knew that. So he held up his head and looked at the sky. Then he stretched out his arms and split his shirt sleeves with his muscles. But about that time he heard old Blind Lemon on the corner, picking his guitar and singing his one-line song:

"I love you, woman, but I don't like yo' low-down ways."

"He blind in de eyes," John Henry said, "but he sho kin see inside my soul." So he put on his hat and started walking around. He walked up and down the street, and then he walked over and stood in front of the Old Ship of Zion Church, where Old Aunt Dinah was leading out her song:

"I'm gonter tawk right straight to Jesus,
    On my knees.
I'm gonter tawk right straight to Jesus,
    On my knees.

LORD, MY BURDEN

Mary, Mark and Luke and John,
All dem prophets dead and gone.
I'm gonter tawk right straight to Jesus,
   On my knees."

And while John Henry was listening to Old Aunt Dinah sing her song, he heard old Hellbuster Henry lay down the word from the pulpit: "And de Lawd told Peter, he say, 'Peter, verily I say unto you, believe in me and lay yo' burden down.'"

"Wonder what was de matter wid Peter?" John Henry said. But before anybody could tell him, Old Aunt Dinah led out another song:

"Seek
  And ye shall find,
Knock
  And de door hit shall be open',
Ask
  And hit shall be given,
When de love come a-twinklin' down."

When John Henry heard that news he held his head up high and walked into the church. "Stand back," he said, "and let me ask old Hellbuster. Hysh up dat singin' and snivelin' around whilst I unrids dis riddle." Then he turned to the preacher and made his say-so:

"Hell-buster," he said, "I'm six foot tall and de fo'ks name me John Henry. I kin outwork any man bawn to die, and ain't nobody kin stop me. I rousts like a fool and I labors like a dog, and I swings me a nine-pound hammer. I comed f'm de Black River country whar de sun don't never shine, and my feets don't tetch de ground. I quit Poor Selma like I was quittin' work, 'cause I knows how to handle my women ———"

"Wait a minute," Hell-buster said. "Don't stand up hyar, braggin'. I knows yo' trouble f'm end to end, and hit ain't no need in tawkin'. You ain't happy or you wouldn't be hyar, makin' such a mannish say-so. Yo' heart is sore and yo' soul is sad. Ain't dat so, John Henry?"

"I'm big and stout," John Henry said, "and men don't git no stouter. I hold my haid up like a natchal man, and I kin tote my burden."

"Tote de burden on yo' back," Hell-buster told John Henry, "and hit ain't a man in dis old town kin shade you wid a burden. But git a burden on yo' heart and watch out whar you wanders."

Then Hell-buster put his eye straight on John

LORD, MY BURDEN

Henry's heart, and he asked him, he said, "Is yo' heart big and stout like yo' shoulders?"

"I'm big all over," John Henry said. "My heart weighs a hund'ed pounds."

"Well, den," said Hell-buster, "how come hit ain't big enough and stout enough to tote de name er Jesus? You's a man, you say, and you won't burn down, but looky yonder at Dinah. So old her teef done growed four times, and all bowed down wid phthisic. She ain't no man and she's old and weak, but she kin tote poor Jesus."

While John Henry was looking at Old Aunt Dinah, all bent over on her crutches, he saw her eyeballs shine like fire, and he heard her sing a new song:

"Oh, ain't I glad?
Yas, ain't I—ain't I glad?
Lawd, ain't I glad, glad,
I got Jesus in my heart."

"I ain't argyin' about all er dat," John Henry told the preacher. "What I wants to know is dis, How kin I shed my burden?"

"Not wid braggin'," Hell-buster said, "and not wid heavy labor. But come up to dis moaners' bench and ask God please to bless you, 'cause God don't keer is you six foot tall, and He don't keer what yo' name is. All God wants is a chance at yo' heart, so's He kin hit you wid de Sperit.

"So come on, all er you sinful men, and come on, you low-down women. You creepers and gamblers and midnight ramblers, come and git to moanin'! Or else God'll set fire to yo' tail and burn you to a cracklin'. Oh, you backsliders and you unbaptized, and you big-tawkin' braggers, git humble in yo' heart and moan and groan yo' sins to Jesus. Oh, sinner, sinner, when de moon drip blood and de sun goes out like a candle—oh, sinner, sinner, when God stops time and Gabriel toots his trumpet—hit's gonter be Glory for all er God's own, but hit'll be hell for de sinners. So git down on yo' knees and moan and ask God to put His hand on you, 'cause hit'll be a Gittin'-up-mawnin' one er dese days, so fare you well, you sinners. Fare you well, you unbaptized, and fare you well, John Henry, 'cause I can't see you when de trumpet sound, and God won't even bother. So git on yo' knees, you liars and moan yo' sins, you creepers. Pray yo' prayer, you gamblin'-man, and give yo' heart to Jesus!"

The gamblers and the liars and the creepers

and thieves came up and started moaning. But big John Henry stood six feet tall and looked straight at Hell-buster.

"Maybe so," John Henry said, "but dat's all for de future. What I comed hyar to find out is how to shed my burden."

About that time Old Aunt Dinah crutched up to John Henry and took him by the right hand. "Git down right hyar, son, on yo' knees, and listen to my say-so. I'll tell you how to ease yo' heart and git yo' peace wid Jesus."

So John Henry got down on his knees and put his head in Old Aunt Dinah's lap, and listened to her say-so.

"John Henry," Old Aunt Dinah said, "I know dat you got trouble. I know yo' path been hard and rough, and I know yo' soul is heavy. But hit's jest one thing which do you like dat, and listen whilst I tell you. You's big and stout and six foot tall, but, son, yo' milk is clabber. Hit's a heap er men ain't stout like you, but dat ain't none er yo'n. Cause God made you stout and He made dem weak, and hit ain't none er yo'n. God made you and He done a good job, but you don't hyar God braggin'. Naw, He leave de braggin' to de fools like you, and goes on and minds

[205]

His business. So bow yo' haid and moan wid me, so God kin git a lick in. And efn He hit you wid de light, He'll sho burn up yo' burden."

So John Henry groveled and moaned until he choked down. Then he stood up and sang:

> "Hyar poor me, on my bended knees,
>   And I don't know what to say.
> But I'm axin' you, won't you please, dear Lawd,
>   Won't you bear my burden away, Lawd, Lawd,
>   Won't you bear my burden away."

When John Henry sang that song, God hit him with the Spirit and knocked him dead. He moaned and groaned and frothed at the mouth, but he couldn't raise his hand. Hell-buster preached him into the Kingdom, and the women gathered around and sang Zion songs, and for forty days and forty nights John Henry was struck dead on the floor.

When he got to his feet he put on his hat. "I been a sinner, but now I'm saved," he told the women. "I comed hyar wid a burden and I laid hit down. So now I'll be a-goin'. So fare you well, my kind friends, and fare you well, Hell-buster, 'cause I got my hat and I'm gittin' around and hit's de last time I will see you."

LORD, MY BURDEN

"Fare you well, my Christian friend," Hell-buster told John Henry. "Hit might turn out jest like you say, but I hopes to git to see you."

So John Henry turned his back on the preacher and walked out of the Old Ship of Zion Church, and he never saw Hell-buster after that. But Hell-buster saw John Henry.

JOHN HENRY LAYS HIS BURDEN DOWN

WHEN John Henry got hit with the Spirit he went back home to Julie Anne. He hung his hat up in the hall and he took her by the right hand. "Darlin'," he said, "maybe you been right and maybe you been wrong, and hit ain't for me to say. I loves you good, but you don't love me, so gimme my workin'-clothes, 'cause I'm a man my size and I works like a man, so I better git to workin'."

"What de matter, darlin'?" Julie Anne said. "You ain't fixin' to quit me?"

"Nawp," said John Henry, "I ain't fixin' to quit you. I done quit, so now I'll git to travelin'. Hit's a heap er cotton on de river, and my hook is gittin' rusty. I know hit's a path to yo' back door and I know somebody been creepin'. But

hit don't weary my mind no more, so I hope
you well and happy."

Then Julie Anne sat down and cried. "Don't
go leave poor me," she said. "Don't go off, John
Henry, 'cause you's my man and I loves you
good and can't nobody change dat. I'm a fool,
maybe, and I done you bad, but God knows
how I love you. You done for me and I done
you bad, but dat's jest 'cause I love you. You
know how hit is, darlin', and you know I can't
tell you. But don't leave me alone all by myse'f,
and maybe I kin show you."

"No mind," John Henry said, " 'cause I ain't
gonter tetch you. I slapped you once, but I
didn't aim to, and hit didn't git me nothin'. So
hand me my hat and my overhalls and let me
git to workin', 'cause work is de onliest thing I
kin do. So fare you well, my darlin'."

Julie Anne got John Henry's clothes, and she
got her hat and bundle. " 'Cause I'm goin' whar-
ever you go," she told her big John Henry.
"Hand in hand, jest like you said when we went
up de river."

"Nawp," John Henry told her. "I'm a man
for work, but I ain't de man which kin make

you happy. So take off yo' hat and take off yo' coat, and don't ever grieve after me."

John Henry walked out of the house and down the street to the river, where cotton was piled for a solid mile and the boats were hauling in more from up the river.

But Julie Anne wouldn't take off her hat and she wouldn't take off her coat. She got her hat and bundle and she lit out right behind John Henry. " 'Cause efn I can wawk wid you hand in hand, I knows I sho kin follow. And ev'y time you turns around you gonter see yo' darlin' standin' wid de tears dreenin' f'm her eyes, 'cause dat's de way I loves you."

But John Henry had put Julie Anne out of his heart and he couldn't hear her talking. So he hunted around for the *Big Jim White* and he asked the driver for a job of work that a man could do, and he pointed to the cotton.

"I ain't braggin'," John Henry said, "but ask dem which knows me who de best cotton-roustin' man, and see if dey don't name me."

The driver looked up and down the river and then he looked at John Henry. "Better go ax de mate," he said, " 'cause I ain't hirin' rousters. I knows you, John Henry, for a roustin' fool, and I sho wisht I had you. But you better go ax de mate for a job, and maybe he will hire you."

John Henry didn't know what to make of that, so he looked straight at the driver. "Unrid dis riddle for me," he said, "and tell me what de matter. How come de driver can't hire me, or else ain't I a rouster? I'm big and black and six foot tall, and I was bawn up on Black River. I loaded cotton for you befo', and I burned out yo' best rollers."

The driver looked at John Henry's hands and then he looked at his feet. "Sho you's big and stout," he said, "and sho you kin roll cotton. Roll or tote, hit's all de same, 'cause you kin shade de best'n'. But you got to tawk to de big old mate, 'cause my heart too sore to tell you."

So John Henry walked up to the mate and said, "Cap'm, I'm John Henry and I comes f'm de Black River country whar de sun don't never shine, and I hyars you needs a rouster. Look at dat old cotton hook, wored clean down wid de hookin'. And look at de cawns in my right hand whar I been rollin' for you."

The mate looked at John Henry, and then he looked at the ground. "Sure I know you, John Henry," the mate said, "and I'll say you are a rouster. You're the best man ever on the *Big Jim White*, and that is saying plenty. But there ain't no job for you today, and maybe not tomorrow, because there've been some changes made down here, and we don't need no rollers."

Then the mate pointed to a donkey engine on the wharf and he pointed to some cable. "Look at that steam winch," he said. "That thing does our rolling. We hook a cable to a bale and one man pulls a lever. That's the way we roll our cotton now, so I guess I can't hire you. That winch rolls cotton like ten good men, and it only takes one nigger."

When John Henry heard that he stood up and laughed and laughed. " 'Scuse me for laughin', Cap'm," he said, "but dat tawk do sound funny. Dat winch might work like ten good men, but how bout John Henry? I burned out all de men you got, and I kin burn dat steam winch out, too.

"So th'ow down another stage for me, so I kin git some action. I'll roll more cotton on de *Big Jim White* den you kin wid dat steam winch, 'cause I'm John Henry and I'm six foot tall and my strenk can't hit de bottom. Maybe de women fool me bad, and maybe, too, de gamblers. Maybe de happy dust cross me up and de preacher put me in de dozens. But rollin' cotton ain't nothin' but work, and can't nobody fool me. So stand back, you bullies, and gimme some room, and watch me roll dat cotton. I'll clean dat boat befo' de sun goes down or my name ain't John Henry."

So everybody stood back and watched while they put down another stage for John Henry, and they talked and bet their money on whether he would burn the winch out.

"Show 'em you's a man," Julie Anne said, "and I puts my money on you. I'm standin' hyar watchin' you work so hard, and bustin' my throat wid rootin'." And then Julie Anne reached down in her stocking-top and took out forty dollars. "I bets dis fawty on my darlin' man," she said, but there were no takers.

But the man at the levers was a nigger named Sam, and he said, "Efn I had de money, I'd fade dat bet, baby, 'cause I'm de man which pull de tail er dis little old steam winch. And I'll burn him out befo' de sun goes down or else I don't want no wages."

So John Henry took his cotton hook in his right hand and Sam caught hold of the lever.

"Hook two bales on de end er my line," Sam

[213]

called to the driver, " 'cause dis old winch jest gittin' hot and she creakin' loud for action."

"Stand out er my way," John Henry said, "and gimme gangway clearance, 'cause I rolls two bales wid dis old hook jest to git my muscles soople."

The sun got high and the day got hot and John Henry started sweating. He kept up with the steam winch, bale for bale. And then the sun got lower. John Henry quit sweating, but he kept right on rolling. The people hoped John Henry would win, so they made up a song to cheer him:

"John Henry was a cotton-rollin' man,
   Had his hook in his hand all de time.
And befo' he'd let dat steam winch burn him down,
   He'd die wid de hook in his hand, Lawd, Lawd,
   'Cause he's rollin' like a natchal man."

When John Henry heard that song he raised up his head and he sang right back:

"I looked at de cotton on de *Big Jim White*,
   Twice as far as I kin see.
Can't see nothin' but my hook in my hand,
   And cotton rollin' after me, Lawd, Lawd,
   And de cotton rollin' after me."

Then John Henry shut his eyes and worked faster than he had ever worked in his life. But his skin wouldn't sweat and his muscles wouldn't slide like rubber. And when he shut his eyes he saw the old woman away up on Black River where the sun don't never shine. She was making charms over a hickory fire and stirring herbs in a kettle.

"Hmmm!" she said, as she chunked the fire. "Ah, Lawd!"

Then John Henry shut his eyes again, and he heard the women singing:

> "By and by, Oh, by and by,
> Gonter lay down my heavy load."

Then the lightning cleaved the air and the sky turned black like night. The Mississippi River ran uphill and the earth shook like a feather. The sun blazed out like a ball of fire, and started to set across the river. And when John Henry saw the sun was about to go down, he reached out with his long cotton hook and stuck it nine inches deep into a bale of cotton.

But when John Henry pulled, the sun went down. And so did big John Henry! The thunder

JOHN HENRY

clapped and the screach-owl screached, and John Henry started talking.

"Hit's nice and quiet and easy to rest," he said, "hyar by de river. Jest lay around in de shade and rest and make tawk wid de old woman. One er dese days I'll git my hat and git on down de river, 'cause I got me a woman name' Julie Anne, and I'll drop 'round to see her."

But he never did. The sun had gone down, and he had gone down with his hook in his hand, and he died rolling cotton.

JOHN HENRY'S LAST GO ROUND

HELL-BUSTER HENRY had on a long black coat the day he preached John Henry's funeral. The Old Ship of Zion Church was full to the doors and all the women were crying. Six tall men brought John Henry in and put him down by the altar. Six more men came marching down, toting his nine-pound hammer. And six more came walking down the aisle, but they couldn't find his cotton hook. Then six young women, all wearing veils, came in and stood beside him.

"How come y'all ladies moanin' so?" Hell-buster asked the women.

So the women stepped out, one by one, and each one spoke her lines:

> "I comed hyar all dressed in red
> 'Cause I hyared John Henry's dead."

JOHN HENRY

"I comed hyar all dressed in green
'Cause he's de best man I ever seen."

"I comed hyar all dressed in blue
'Cause I loved John Henry true."

"I comed hyar all dressed in gray
'Cause Cold Death tuck my man away."

"I comed hyar all dressed in yaller
'Cause John Henry quit Poor Selma."

Then the last woman didn't say a word. She stepped out and took off her veil, and she was Poor Selma!

She looked at the preacher and then she looked at John Henry. "Lay down, darlin'," she said, "and git yo' rest. You quit me when I wanted you bad and tuck up wid another woman. Now yo's stretched out cold in death, but yo' yuther gal ain't hyar moanin'. So rest yo' time out, my lovin' man, and when you gits to Glory you gonter find me standin' by yo' side, and den maybe you will love me."

Then Hell-buster got up and said, "Efn hit's any er dis poor man's kind friends would like to say a word, all right, let's hyar you."

JOHN HENRY'S LAST GO ROUND

'And when Hell-buster said that, a thousand niggers from the Yellow Dog railroad came up and stood beside the coffin. Then old man Billie Bob Russell came up and stood at the head of the coffin. "Now when I drop my hat," he said, "you niggers open up and say just what you want to."

Then old man Billie Bob Russell dropped his hat and a thousand niggers opened up their mouths and sang:

> "John Henry was a hammer-swingin' man.
> Burned out dat nigger named Sam.
> And efn dat ain't swingin' like a natchal man,
> Well den, I'll be damn, Lawd, Lawd,
> Well den, I'll be damn."

When the Yellow Dog railroad niggers sang that they sat down and moaned for John Henry. Then up walked a thousand roustabouts from the *Big Jim White*, with the driver at their head. "Y'all niggers line out and lock hands," the driver said, "and let me hyar some racket. Rattle dem words like a loadin'-line and moan jest like dat whistle. So come on, you bullies, and sing dis song, 'cause you all knowed John Henry."

JOHN HENRY

The roustabouts opened their mouths wide
and sang:

"John Henry was a cotton-rollin' man,
  Had his hook in his hand all de time.
And befo' he'd let dat steam winch burn him down,
  He died wid his hook in his hand, Lawd, Lawd,
  And he died wid his hook in his hand."

When the rousters sat down and started moaning, Old Aunt Dinah crutched up to the casket,
and sang:

"John Henry made his troubles easy,
  On his knees.
John Henry made his troubles easy,
  On his knees.
John Henry got down on his knees,
And said, Jesus, he'p me, please.
John Henry made his troubles easy,
  On his knees."

When Old Aunt Dinah sat down and started
moaning, Hell-buster Henry got up and took a
drink of water. He looked at the ceiling and then
he looked at John Henry.

"John Henry," he said, "dar you lay all cold
in death, and hyar stand me a-tawkin'. I 'mem-

bers when you come hyar de yuther day and I hit you wid de Sperit. All er dese ladies moans after you, and all de men say you's a good'n', 'cause dey stands and sings about how you works and how you died a-rollin'. And so I reads de Word to you and give yo' soul some comfort. 'Well done, my faithful servant; rest from yo' weary labor.' From what I hyars you was a man built outn bone and muscle. You had yo' troubles hyar below, and now you's up to Glory.

"Yes, John Henry, you was a man, but God done knocked you over. And you ain't nothin' but a dab er clay away back on Black River. Hit's dark up dar cause de sun don't shine, and I hopes you's feelin' pleasant. Dey weeps and moans and sings yo' praise, but all er dat stuff don't count, 'cause when you died all er dat died, and hit ain't no more John Henry.

"But, John Henry, you didn't die; you jest laid down yo' burden. You was a man, but women and steam was jest a little bit too many. But don't you worry and don't you fret, 'cause when de Sperit hit you hit knocked de work and hit knocked de gals like a skyrocket at Christmas."

Then the old woman from the Black River

country stepped up and stood before Hell-buster. She looked at him, then she looked at the floor, and then she looked out the window. "John Henry," she said, "you was a man, but didn't tote yo' burden. Work, yas, you done all er dat, but you couldn't handle women. You had a good woman named Julie Anne, but you let her eat yo' heart out. Yo' burden put you on yo' knees, and now old Cold Death got you. So fare you well, my little son. I'll meet you on Black River."

"You's sayin' a lie," Poor Selma said, " 'cause dat gal didn't love him. He done for her and she done him bad, and dat's what stretched him out."

"Don't go lyin' in dis church," Hell-buster Henry told her. "Efn dat gal loved John Henry so, why ain't she hyar moanin'?"

"Don't lie on de dead," Old Aunt Dinah said. "Don't you know de Ten Commandments? 'So you reads on down to a Number Ten, and you lie on de dead and you's doin' a sin.' So may God strike you over."

But the old woman from the Black River country stood up and said. "John Henry loved his Julie Anne and she loved John Henry. Bofe had they faults, but dat didn't hurt, only dey couldn't git together. John Henry liked to work and brag, and Julie Anne liked to trifle. But hit didn't keep 'em f'm lovin' each other, and I'm de one which knows hit. Julie Anne plagued John Henry bad, but John Henry plagued her, too."

"Sayin' don't make hit so," Poor Selma told her. "Why ain't Julie Anne at de church, a-moanin' for her lover?"

The old woman looked at Poor Selma and then she looked at John Henry. "I'll show you," she said, and she held up her right hand and said, "Come on, Sam, like I told you."

Then the nigger named Sam came walking down, toting a heavy bundle. He laid it down by John Henry's side, and raised up the blanket.

"Dat's Julie Anne, all cold in death," the old woman told them. "We found her wid John Henry's hook in her hand, layin' by a bale er cotton. She seed John Henry go down, last night, and so she followed after."

When the old woman said that, all the niggers from the Yellow Dog railroad and all the rousters from the *Big Jim White*, and all the moaning women stood up and sang a song:

[223]

JOHN HENRY

"John Henry had him a pretty little wife,
    And her name was Julie Anne.
She picked up de hook John Henry laid down,
    She rolled cotton like a natchal man, Lawd, Lawd,
    And she died wid his hook in her hand."

Then Hell-buster raised his right hand and said the words over John Henry and Julie Anne. "Ashes unto ashes, Lawd, and dust unto dust. John Henry was a man, and Julie Anne was a woman. So fare you well, fare you well.

"I kin see you now, wawkin' side by side in Glory. John Henry died like a natchal man and Julie Anne died like a woman. So lock yo' hands and flap yo' wings, 'cause I'm preachin' you in de Kingdom.

"Saint Peter, give John Henry a crown as tall as a John B. Stutson, and fix Julie Anne up wid some wings and a harp and a pair er golden slippers. Now march on down to de Throne er Grace and set at de Welcome Table!

"Oh, John Henry, why don't you eat? Hit's pyore milk and honey. And efn you don't like dat kind er grub, Saint Peter, bring him some cabbage. Bring him some turnip greens tree-top high and a big pan full er cawnbread. Oh, Julie

JOHN HENRY'S LAST GO ROUND

Anne, what do you want? Yo's wid yo' John
Henry. I kin see you smile and take his right
hand and put yo' haid on his right shoulder. I
kin see de Lawd smile down on you and give bofe
his blessin': 'Well done, well done, my faithful
friends. Rest from yo' weary labor.'

"Oh, you sinners, can't you see dat pair all
r'ared back in Glory? How you gonter git dar
wid yo' sinnin' ways and set at de Welcome
Table? You better quit yo' gamblin' and quit
yo' ramblin' and git right like John Henry. Oh,
you low-down women, you triflin' women, can't
you see Julie Anne up yonder? How you gonter
git dar wid yo' friv'lin' ways, when you know
old Satan's got you. You bears false witness on
yo' friends and unlocks yo' back door to de
creepers. Oh, you'll never git to heaven like Julie
Anne onless you quits yo' low-down livin'.

"So come on, you liars, and come on, you
gamblers, and come on, you low-down women;
git down on yo' knees, and git yo' heart right,
and give yo' soul to Jesus, 'cause dat's how John
Henry and Julie Anne done when de burden got
too heavy."

THE END

[225]

JOHN HENRY *by* Roark Bradford
Set up in Linotype Garamond
Original woodcuts by J. J. Lankes
Format by A. W. Rushmore
Manufactured by the Haddon Craftsmen
Published by The Literary Guild, *New York*

ROARK BRADFORD

AND HIS BOOKS

———————•

"He can draw the Negro he knows in single situations that reveal him with a power of insight and a magic in his touch that no one else has come near."
—*Louisville Courier-Journal*

Roark Bradford is amply qualified to write about the Negro. He was born on a plantation near the Mississippi River, fifteen miles from a railroad. He had a Negro for a nurse and Negroes for playmates when he was growing up. He has seen them at work in the fields, in the levee camps, and on the river. He knows them in their homes, in church, at their picnics and their funerals. After acquiring an LL.B. degree at the University of California he entered a training-camp at the outbreak of the war, and after the Armistice various post-war assignments kept him in the army until 1920. Since the war he has worked on newspapers in Atlanta and New Orleans. In 1927 he decided to devote all his time to writing fiction, and his second published story, *Child of God*, received the O. Henry Memorial award.

From the Reviews of
OL' MAN ADAM
AN' HIS CHILLUN'
The book on which "The Green Pastures" was based

The New York Times

"*Ol' Man Adam an' His Chillun'* is a collection of Negro biblical interpretations; they are vastly amusing; but they are the product of a Christian outlook so primitive that it will not be long before they are as unique as the Uncle Remus animal tales; yet it would not be an unapt characterization of Mr. Bradford's book to say that it belongs in the same category with *Uncle Remus*. Those who do not look into the volume can be only those unacquainted with *Uncle Remus*, or, if acquainted, lacking appreciation of exotic and strangely flavored yarns."

The Chicago Post

"Not since *Uncle Remus* has there been a book like this. Needless to say, the book is howlingly funny. Yet it is sincere, and certainly represents a real point of view. Like the Uncle Remus books, it presents real folklore, although with a biblical basis."

The Philadelphia Record

"Mr. Bradford has had the idea of setting down a connected series of biblical stories as they are told by devout Negroes. With only a few exceptions all are from the Old Testament, just as spirituals usually have Old Testament themes. Indeed the stories are prose first-cousins to many of the spirituals and must be read with much the same approach as that with which we hear the songs. If these stories, irresistibly funny though they are, are read simply as funny stories, most of their power will be missed."